KILL OR BE KILLED

Chet Walker returns to Kansas when his brother Burt faces trouble at the Flying W. Chet, after five years in Montana, accepts that Burt won the girl they both love, but he's unprepared for the trouble awaiting him. He becomes the target of gunfire as soon as he arrives. It seems that every man's hand is against him as he fights back. He must survive the mayhem and confront the crooks behind the plot to take over the range.

Books by Corba Sunman
in the Linford Western Library:

RANGE WOLVES
LONE HAND
GUN TALK
TRIGGER LAW
GUNSMOKE JUSTICE
BIG TROUBLE
GUN PERIL
SHOWDOWN AT SINGING SPRINGS
TWISTED TRAIL
RAVEN'S FEUD
FACES IN THE DUST
MARSHAL LAW
ARIZONA SHOWDOWN
THE LONG TRAIL
SHOOT-OUT AT OWL CREEK
RUNNING CROOKED
HELL'S COURTYARD

CORBA SUNMAN

KILL OR
BE KILLED

Complete and Unabridged

LINFORD
Leicester

First published in Great Britain in 2008 by
Robert Hale Limited
London

First Linford Edition
published 2009
by arrangement with
Robert Hale Limited
London

British Library CIP Data

Sunman, Corba.
    Kill or be killed - - (Linford western library)
    1. Western stories.
    2. Large type books.
    I. Title II. Series
    823.9'2–dc22

    ISBN 978–1–84782–777–7

Published by
F. A. Thorpe (Publishing)
Anstey, Leicestershire

Set by Words & Graphics Ltd.
Anstey, Leicestershire
Printed and bound in Great Britain by
T. J. International Ltd., Padstow, Cornwall

This book is printed on acid-free paper

1

Chet Walker reined in on the crest of the slope overlooking Coyote Creek in Pearson County, West Kansas, and sat motionless on his black horse as he looked over the small cow-spread where he had been born twenty-five years before. A thin sliver of the moon in its first quarter enabled him to see the well-remembered features of the creek but threw dense shadows into the hollows and low ground. The range was silent, still, seemingly holding its breath awaiting his return, and Walker was choked by a stream of memories of his early life in the big cabin by the creek. His harsh, angular features, shadowed under the low brim of his black Stetson, tightened into even deeper lines and his cold brown eyes narrowed into slits.

The black, sensing the end of the trail, was ready for a feed, and shook its

1

head as it took an impatient step down the slope towards the cabin. Walker checked it abruptly. There was a light in the cabin window and he had no intention of riding in cold maybe to collect a slug for his unannounced intrusion. When he rode out five years earlier he had left under a cloud, and his elder brother, Burt, had told him never to return, but he had received word from Burt only four weeks before, asking him to come back because there was more trouble than he could handle.

Chet had worked as a deputy sheriff in Montana for the past three years, but quit when Burt's message reached him. Sheriff Grimmer had been loath to lose him but Chet would not stay, so Grimmer asked him to drop into the state marshal's office in Kansas City on his way home. Chet had done so, and Marshal Hicks had persuaded him to become a deputy state marshal with the chore of checking out the burgeoning trouble in Pearson County.

'I had a deputy marshal, Bill Wymer,

working under cover in Pearson County, trying to get at the roots of the trouble,' Hicks had said. 'I got word last week that he was murdered — shot in the back; and you going home after five years would provide good cover. Will you take a badge?'

Chet had agreed, and carried the shield-shaped law badge in his breast pocket when he left Kansas City. Now he was back on home range and wondering what had gone wrong for Burt to call for help. He sighed heavily, touched spurs to the black's flanks, and rode down the slope. He opened the gate to the yard without dismounting, and, as he crossed to the front of the cabin, the light inside the building was extinguished.

He heard the sound of a window being opened. He reined in, tall in the saddle, wide-shouldered and powerfully built.

'Who is out there?' a harsh voice demanded. 'Speak up quick. I got a rifle on you and my trigger finger is real nervous.'

'I'm Chet Walker,' he replied, 'and who are you? You don't sound like my brother Burt.'

'Chet, by God! Is it really you? This is Dave Sawtell. Do you remember me? I ride for Circle B, but Sue Bartram put me in here when Burt was shot last week.'

'Is Burt dead?' The news hit Chet in the pit of the stomach with the stunning shock of a mule's kick. He stepped down from his horse and trailed his reins.

'No, he ain't dead yet, but I reckon he's knocking at the gate. Hold on. I'll relight the lamp and open the door. I'm sorry about the welcome, but a man can't be too careful these days.'

The word of Burt's shooting seemed to freeze Chet's thoughts. He saw lamplight flare inside the cabin, then the door was thrown open and a tall, thin figure appeared in the doorway with a rifle clasped and ready for action in capable hands. He recognized the face that was illuminated by the yellow light.

'Howdy, Chet?' Sawtell's voice was pitched low. 'Long time no see! Say, I'm real sorry about Burt.'

'What happened to him?' Walker's thin lips barely moved as he framed the question. Marshal Hicks had warned of big trouble around here, but it seemed he had been understating the situation.

'Bushwhacked as he rode back from town last Saturday night. I was talking to him only minutes before he left, and he said he was looking forward to seeing you again. He was found Sunday morning with a bullet in his back, and Doc Pryce is looking after him in Flat Ridge. It was a helluva thing to happen.'

'So what's the trouble around here?' Chet's tight, unemotional tone gave no indication of his feelings. 'I'm here because Burt called me back to side him.'

'Take a look around the range and you won't find hide or hair of a Flying W cow anywhere. Burt was cleaned out a month gone, and would have quit then but for Sue. She wouldn't let him pull stakes, and she put it into his mind to send for you. Say, you better come in and I'll give you the whole story. Did you know Burt was fixing to wed Sue?'

'Five years ago I was expecting to marry Sue,' Chet replied. 'I rode out when Burt said he was interested in her, so why haven't they wed? What's kept them waiting so long? I thought they would have tied the knot years ago.'

'Sue ain't in love with Burt and never has been.' Sawtell turned and stepped aside for Chet to enter the cabin. 'Heck, you've growed some since I last seen you,' he observed. 'We heard about you taking up law work in Montana and making a pretty good job of it. I guess you'll need all the skill you can muster to sort out the trouble that's come to this range.'

'Is Abe Curry still the county sheriff?' Chet demanded.

'Yeah, but he ain't the man he was. All I ever hear him do these days is threaten to retire. He can't handle his job properly, and everybody knows it. That's why the range has got lawless. The bad men have grabbed the upper hand.'

'Can you put names to those who have given Burt trouble?'

Sawtell shook his head, looking suddenly uneasy. He was aged about thirty, had an open face and seemed genuinely worried by local events.

'Chet, I guess you need to talk to Sheriff Curry about that. It ain't for me to go naming men I suspect, because I don't know anything — only heard what's been said by others. Did you hear Hank Bartram was killed about six months ago?'

'No!' Chet shook his head, deeply shocked by the news for Sue's father had always seemed indestructible. 'Did they get his killer?'

'No. It's still a mystery after all this time, the same as who robbed the bank and held up the Wells Fargo stage line last year. There's a gang operating in

7

these parts and they're pretty good at the job. A deputy state marshal came in recently, and was killed before he could get a lead on the bad 'uns. That's how tough it is.'

'So who is running Circle B now Hank is dead?'

'Alice Bartram married Rafe Colby, and he took over the reins when Hank was killed. The Circle B ain't a pleasant place to work any more. I figured Colby didn't know anything at all about cattle ranching, but he seems to be making the ranch pay. Mind you, he's hired a couple of hardcase gunnies to protect the place — Chuck Hackett and Don Farris, and Curry ain't able to keep them in their rightful place. They ride roughshod around the county and seem to cause more trouble than the bad men they are supposed to fight. Most of the old crew at Circle B pulled out when the gunnies came in. Sue and Alice ain't got a friendly face around them, except for me, and I don't know how much longer I can last.'

'Rafe Colby,' Chet mused. 'Is that the same Colby who set up as a gambler in the Red Dog saloon in Flat Ridge just before I rode away five years ago?'

'You got it in one.' Sawtell nodded. 'When Colby met up with Alice Bartram she must have seen the stars in his eyes because they didn't waste any time getting hitched. She sure knew what she wanted, but I don't think she is a happy woman these days. Colby must be hell to live with, and he's got those two gunnies living on the ranch. They got no respect for a woman, throw their weight around among the crew, and that's why most of the old hands have up and left; they didn't like the conditions they had to work under.'

Chet opened his mouth to make an observation but snapped his teeth together as the sound of a number of running horses reached his ears. Sawtell heard the disturbance in the same moment and dropped a hand to the butt of the pistol in his holster. He turned swiftly, blew out the lamp, and darkness swooped into the cabin.

'Better get your head down,' Sawtell warned. 'That bunch has been through here a couple of times before, and they usually toss a few slugs at the cabin in passing.'

Chet dropped to one knee as gunfire erupted and a spate of slugs smacked into the front wall of the cabin. Voices were yelling outside. Chet drew his pistol and edged towards the nearest window to peer out into the night, gun uplifted and cocked.

He saw shadowy figures galloping through the yard and estimated six riders were in the group. Gun flashes ripped the shadows apart and bullets slammed into the thick front wall of the cabin, one slug smashing the window where Chet was standing. He ducked flying glass but felt the sharp pain of a shard slicing into his right cheek. He opened the window, pushed his gun muzzle through the aperture, and fired without seeming to aim. The rider who had fired into the window gave a yell, fell forward over the neck of his horse, and then pitched out of the saddle to thump on the hard ground.

The riders swept around to the back of the cabin and disappeared from sight. The sound of their passing receded and silence returned. The lone figure sprawled in the dust of the yard did not move, and Chet felt his way to the door, his teeth clenched and his gun ready for more action.

'I got one of them,' he remarked grimly. 'Let's go take a look at him.'

'Hell, you shouldn't have fired at them!' Sawtell gasped.

'They were shooting at us,' Chet replied, 'and any of their slugs could have killed either one of us. In my book it was self-defence. Light the lamp again and we'll take a look at what I got. I'm mighty curious about men who ride in the night shooting indiscriminately at innocent folk.'

Sawtell relit the lamp and followed Chet out to the yard, the lamp held high. The light was not strong, but good enough to reveal the face of the dead man sprawled in the dust, who was a stranger to Chet.

'Do you know him?' Chet demanded.

'Hell! You bet I know him!' Sawtell spoke in a shocked whisper. 'It's Floyd Carson. His pa, Ben Carson, bought out Elmer Brooks three years ago when Brooks gave up ranching. Jeez! What was Floyd doing with that back-shooting pack of hellions? It doesn't make sense that a youngster with such a rich father would waste his time with a bunch of bullies. But Floyd ain't done a day's work since he's been in the county. He was always seeking pleasure and excitement, and now he's dead.'

'He must have had a warped sense of pleasure, riding around with hell-raisers,' Chet commented. 'This ain't the first time the place has been shot up, huh? So Floyd Carson is a part of the trouble hereabouts.'

'There'll be hell to pay over this!' Sawtell shook his head. 'I wouldn't want to be the one who has to tell Ben

Carson his son is dead. Ben never looks easy to get along with.'

'I think you'd better ride back to Circle B and leave this mess to me,' Chet mused. 'I'll take Floyd's body into Flat Ridge and talk to the sheriff. You don't need to get involved in this, Dave. I'll handle it. Someone shot Burt in the back and I mean to get whoever did it. This is my fight and I'll handle it my way. When you get back to Circle B just let Sue know I'm back.'

'I ain't gonna argue with you,' Sawtell said, obviously scared by what had occurred. 'Sue won't like it when I show up at Circle B, but I ain't no gunslinger, and I draw the line at shooting folks, bad men or otherwise.'

Chet nodded, and crossed to a saddle horse standing by the fence around the yard. He led the animal to where Floyd Carson's body was lying and hoisted the cadaver across the saddle.

'I'll head into town now,' he told Sawtell. 'You better get out of here soon as you can. The place can take care of itself. There's nothing of value around here. So long, Dave! Tell Sue I'll be out to Circle B soon as I can make it. I sure need to talk to her.'

'Be careful how you ride in when you come,' Sawtell warned. 'Colby's gunnies don't take well to strangers showing up.'

'It sounds like they are in need of a lesson in manners,' Chet retorted.

He fetched his black, swung into the saddle, and led the horse carrying the corpse as he rode out on the trip to Flat Ridge. The night was not totally dark and he easily followed the well-defined trail across the range. Two hours of steady riding found him on a crest overlooking the town, and he reined in to gaze down at the cluster of yellow lights which marked the main street. He was keenly aware that five years had slipped by since he had last looked at Flat Ridge.

His thoughts were stark as he rode into the town but he forced them into the back of his mind. He had no time for mooning over the past. There was bad trouble here and his job was to get to grips with it. He reined up in front of the law office and paused to look around. A lot of noise was coming from the Red Dog saloon, although the time was pushing towards midnight, and the street was still crowded, as if the townsfolk thought there would be no tomorrow. A sigh ripped through him when he caught glimpses of the shadowy town he had once known so well, and he was aware that the past could easily haunt him.

He dismounted and wrapped the reins of both horses around the hitch rail in front of the law office. Two men were standing in the shadows in front of the closed office door, and one of them was smoking a cigarette, the red end of which brightened as he drew on it. Both men moved aside as Chet stepped on to the sidewalk.

'Say, is that a dead man across that saddle?' one of them demanded.

'As far as I know only dead men ride

face down,' Chet countered. 'Is the sheriff here?'

'No, Curry is out of town on a trip,' said the man smoking the cigarette. 'I'm Lance Decker, the deputy sheriff. I'm running the law around here until Curry gets back. Who are you, mister, and what are you doing with a dead man?'

'The name is Chet Walker, and the dead man was one of six riders who charged through Flying W on Coyote Creek like a bunch of Indians. They shot the hell out of the cabin and I downed this one before they left.'

'The hell you say!' Decker exclaimed, suddenly becoming animated. 'Who is the stiff?'

'I got no idea.' Chet shook his head. 'I never saw him before. I've been away about five years, and he wasn't around before I left.'

Decker stepped off the sidewalk and went to the horse carrying Floyd Carson. He struck a match, held its flickering light close to the dead man's head, and uttered an imprecation when he recognized the stiff features. He dropped the lighted match with a curse when it burned his fingers.

'By God, it's Floyd Carson!' He spoke in a hoarse, shocked tone. 'Jeez, there'll be hell to pay when Ben Carson gets to hear about this!' He turned to the man standing motionless on the sidewalk, 'Sam, you'd better fork your bronc out to C7 and tell Ben his son is dead.'

The man departed almost at a run, his boots pounding heavily on the sidewalk.

'Come into the office and tell me what happened,' Decker said. 'I need to make a report on this.'

'That will have to wait,' Chet said firmly. 'I heard that my brother Burt was shot in the back last Saturday night and is at the doc's house. I'll check him out and then come back to you.'

'Suit yourself.' Decker shrugged. He was a big man with broad shoulders, and looked as wide as a barn door in the shadows. 'But you better not get caught alone when Ben Carson rides in. He ain't gonna take kindly to the man who killed his son.'

'Maybe he should have brought up his son to act differently around folks,' Chet declared. 'I'd like to know what Floyd was doing riding with a pack of trigger-happy galoots. He almost caught me with a slug, which is why I brought him down.'

Decker did not reply. He turned to the law office door and opened it, then paused and glanced at Chet.

'You better be back here before Ben rides in,' he warned.

Chet turned away when the deputy entered the office. He untied his horse, swung into the saddle, and rode along the street towards the doctor's house where a light was burning in the front window of the medical office. He wrapped his reins around a post in the picket fence and walked to the door, a sense of eagerness seizing him at the thought of seeing Burt again. He knocked loudly, and the door was opened almost immediately by a short, fleshy, middle-aged man whom Chet remembered well.

'Howdy, Doc?' Chet greeted. 'I heard about Burt getting shot and that you're taking care of him. I always reckoned you were the best doctor in the world. How is Burt?'

'Chet Walker!' A wide grin appeared on Doc Pryce's fleshy features. 'Thank God you've arrived! I've been watching for you more than a week now. Burt is pulling through. It is a slow job, but the sight of you will give him a big boost. Come on in.'

Pryce stuck out a hand and Chet grasped and shook it warmly. He entered the house as Pryce stepped aside, closed the door and slid home a bolt.

'I'm taking no chances,' Pryce said. 'I got the feeling that whoever shot Burt in the back might make another try to finish him off. It's a bad business, and the situation around here is deteriorating daily. It's getting so it's not safe to walk through the town day or night. Abe Curry is well past doing his job properly these days, and what we need is a new sheriff who can handle the law dealing. Say, you got blood on your face! Have you found trouble already?'

Chet explained his homecoming and saw the doctor's face turn pale when he learned of Floyd Carson's death.

'That's the last thing we needed around here.' Pryce shook his head. 'I saw Floyd in town earlier this evening — him and that no-good bunch he hangs out with. He's been a hell-raiser ever since his family moved into the county — one of those young men who has too much of everything and thinks the whole world belongs to him. He drank and gambled too much, and killed two men who crossed his path. Ben Carson, his father, could see no wrong in Floyd. He reckoned the boy was just growing up. Floyd should have been made to work on the C7, but he had too much money and not enough discipline to keep him straight. But you can't tell that to Ben.'

'So mebbe Floyd was on his way back to C7 from town and decided to raise a little hell at Flying W.' Chet frowned. 'He must have known Burt was here in town. I found Dave Sawtell keeping an eye on Flying W when I arrived there. Have you got any idea who might have been riding with Floyd tonight? There was a bunch of about six of them shooting up the cabin on Coyote Creek, and it looked like they meant to hit anyone inside.'

'Like I said, Floyd has been running around with a tough bunch, all hell-raisers.' Pryce shook his head. 'I don't like this situation one bit. I reckon Ben Carson will be looking for you when he hears about Floyd, and he's not a man to listen to reason. If you asked me for advice, Chet, I'd say without hesitation that you should mount up and ride as far away from here as possible and don't come back. Ben Carson will be after your blood, and he won't rest until he's sent you in

Floyd's footsteps to the Great Beyond!'

'I'd like to see Burt now,' Chet said quietly. 'Has he said anything about when he was shot?'

'Not a word. He's having a tough fight, but he's making some progress. I guess he's been waiting for you to get back. I'll take you up to his room. He's probably asleep now, so don't rouse him. You'll need to come back tomorrow to talk to him. I'll let him know you've arrived and prepare him to meet you.'

Chet followed the doctor up to a back bedroom and saw Burt lying asleep in a bed. He was shocked by his brother's pale, gaunt face. Burt had been a powerful man, but the bullet that brought him down had almost killed him, and his physical condition had suffered greatly in his struggle to recover. He seemed almost a stranger with his sunken cheeks and unhealthy pallor.

'He's looking a lot better now,' Pryce observed. 'He's a real fighter, Chet, and

I give him a good chance of making a full recovery, but it was touch and go for a week. He only regained consciousness two days ago, and has hardly uttered a word, but I can see him improving day by day.'

Chet approached the bed and placed a gentle hand on Burt's forehead to find the flesh hot and clammy. Burt was breathing heavily; snoring gently. The room reeked of whatever the doc was using to treat the wound and the sickly smell was cloying and unsavoury.

'I'm wondering who shot him in the back,' Chet mused. 'And I'm sure as hell gonna find out before I get through around here. I'll be back in the morning to talk to him when he's awake, Doc.'

'I reckon by tomorrow morning you'll be up to your neck in bad trouble,' Pryce warned. 'You better listen to what I'm telling you, Chet. Ben Carson is gonna want your blood no matter the reason why you killed his boy. That's the kind of man he is. You won't be able to talk with him. He'll be gunning for you, so you should put a lot of distance between yourself and this town as soon as you can.'

'I ain't running anywhere,' Chet replied. 'I've come back to fight whatever trouble there is. If Ben Carson wants a fight he'll find me ready, willing and able. Thanks for the advice, Doc. I appreciate it, but you must see there's nothing I can do but play the hand that's been dealt me, come hell or high water.'

'I was afraid you'd take that attitude.' Pryce shook his head. 'The trouble around here has been slow in building up, but all it needs right now is a flame to light the fuse and blow the whole business into an inferno and I guess you're the one to set it going. The explosion has got to come and it could be mighty costly, for when killing starts it never seems to know when to stop.'

'Thanks for taking good care of Burt, Doc.' Chet closed his mind to the doctor's warning. 'I'll be back in the morning.'

'I wish you'd listen to me,' Pryce urged. 'I'd hate to dig slugs out of you.'

'I'll take my chances.' Chet opened the door to depart and instantly the shadows surrounding the house were tattered by orange gun-flame and the raucous booming of Colt-fire.

2

Chet dropped to the ground instinctively and rolled to his right out of the doorway. He got up on his elbows, pistol in his hand. His ears rang from the crash of the shots, but by the time he was ready to fight the shooting was over, and he lay listening to the fading echoes, his gun cocked and poised. He heard the sound of receding footsteps out there in the night. Silence returned slowly, and he clenched his teeth as he remembered hearing Doc Pryce cry out as the shooting erupted.

He sprang to his feet, eyes narrowed, watching for trouble. When nothing untoward occurred he eased in through the open door of the house to find the doctor stretched out on the floor with a spreading patch of blood on his right shoulder. Chet holstered his pistol and dropped to one knee. Doc's eyelids were fluttering and he was moaning, his fleshy face ghastly pale in shock.

'Doc, can you hear me?' Chet demanded. 'Come on, speak to me.'

Pryce opened his eyes. He stared up at Chet for a moment, and then animation seeped into his gaze.

'I've been shot!' he gasped. 'Help me up, Chet, so I can check the wound. It doesn't feel so bad. Maybe I'll live.'

'Who is gonna take the slug out of you?' Chet demanded. 'You're the only doctor within a hundred miles.'

'Bill Newton here in town is a horse doctor. He can take out a slug if it ain't too bad.' Pryce groaned as Chet eased him to his feet and then half-carried him into the room which was used as a surgery. 'Put me down on the couch,' Pryce gasped.

Chet complied, and watched the doctor's skilled fingers examining the wound.

'The slug is in there,' Pryce observed, 'and it will have to come out.'

'Where does Bill Newton live?' Chet

demanded. 'I'll fetch him.'

'He's got a house three doors away to the right,' Pryce replied. He paused when a voice at the front door called his name. 'That sounds like Decker, the deputy,' he observed. 'Bring him in, Chet.'

Chet went to the front door to find Decker standing on the threshold, a gun in his hand. The deputy's large face was filled with an expression of anticipation.

'Where's the doc?' Decker demanded. 'I heard shots, and saw this door open. Is Doc all right?'

'He's been shot,' Chet replied, and led the way back into the office, followed closely by Decker.

'It looks like you'll live,' Decker remarked after taking a close look at Doc's wound. 'So what happened?'

'Jawing about it can wait,' Pryce replied. 'Get me Bill Newton. He'll have to remove the slug.'

Decker grimaced and departed. Chet gazed at Pryce, his mind seething with conjecture.

'I wonder which of us that ambusher was after,' he mused.

Pryce gazed at him, his eyes narrowing as he said: 'I assumed he was after you, Chet.' He stifled a groan of pain. 'Why should anyone want to shoot me?'

'If I could answer that question I'd be a whole lot wiser than I am right now, Doc. But no one knows I'm back in the county yet, so I reckon the shots were meant for you.'

'I've got no enemies!' Pryce shook his head. 'A doctor is a valuable man in any community. If someone gets himself shot these days the first man he wants to see is the local doctor. I'm here to help anyone who needs my skill. No, Chet, I think someone was after you. Burt was shot last week, and now you're the main target.'

Chet grimaced. 'I'm considering Burt's shooting,' he said grimly. 'Someone is out to get Coyote Creek and the Flying W, that's obvious. The range has already been stripped of cattle, so I need to find the man who is interested in buying the spread and hear what he has to say.'

'You reckon it will be that easy?' Pryce stifled a groan and slumped back on the couch with sweat beading his forehead.

'Hell no!' Chet shook his head. 'I'll probably wind up dead before I get anywhere near to who is behind this business, but I'm hoping Burt can tell me something of what's been going on around here.'

'Say, do you think whoever did the shooting was after Burt again?' Pryce asked.

'That's a thought.' Chet turned to face the door of the room when he heard voices outside.

Decker returned, accompanied by Bill Newton, a tall, thin man in shirtsleeves whose sparse brown hair was tousled. Newton blinked rapidly in the lamplight, like an owl which had been suddenly awakened.

'So someone caught up with you at last, huh?' Newton demanded, chuckling with grim humour. He bent over the prostrate doctor and examined the wound. 'Yes, you'll live,' he went on. 'I'll have to take that bullet out. Did you catch the gunnie?'

'He was long gone by the time I arrived,' Decker replied. 'Can you manage on your own, Bill? I need to get a couple of statements from Walker. There's been hell to pay since he got back in the county.'

'I can handle this,' Newton replied. 'You two get out of here.'

Decker seemed anxious to leave and led the way out to the street. He paused and looked around into the shadows as if expecting more shooting, but the night was dark and silent. Chet joined the deputy, his thoughts fast-moving, and led his horse as they walked to the law office.

'Do you get much trouble around town?' Chet enquired.

'Not in town itself. The law department is on its toes. Nobody gets away with anything around here. But it's a different story out there on the range.'

'So who shot my brother Burt last week?' Chet countered.

'I got no idea. He was ambushed out on the trail. He didn't see anyone or anything, so he said, and the ambusher got clean away. You've been a lawman up in Montana, I hear, so you know how it works. If someone picks his mark well and leaves no clues then it's impossible to get a line on him.'

'But the general situation should throw up a few pointers,' Chet said. 'Who around here is interested in taking over Coyote Creek? All Flying W stock has been rustled, and now it seems the range is up for grabs.'

'There are a number of men around the county who might be interested in your place, but nobody has showed his hand yet. It's a case of waiting and watching. Soon as who ever is behind this trouble tips his hand then we will move in.' Decker paused at the law office door and felt in his pockets for a key.

He was unlocking the door and Chet

was wrapping his reins around a rail when the sound of hoofs rattled on the street. Chet moved into the shadows against the front wall of the office as six riders appeared, approaching at a canter. Chet dropped his right hand to the butt of his gun. He figured it was too soon for Ben Carson to put in an appearance and wondered who was out riding at midnight.

The riders came towards the law office. Decker opened the office door and a bright shaft of yellow light stabbed out across the street. Chet, his eyes narrowed to pierce the gloom, felt his pulse race when he recognized Dave Sawtell in the group. Then his gaze fell upon the woman at Sawtell's side and his teeth clicked together. Sue Bartram had not changed much in the five years which had elapsed since Chet last saw her, and he stifled some bitter thoughts as he recalled that once they had talked of marriage. The lamplight issuing from the law office bathed her as brightly as if the sun was shining, and Chet saw even the smallest detail about her. She was a tall girl with dark hair, and her expression showed she still had an aggressive manner. Her stubborn chin was thrust out as if she was ready to take on the whole world.

Chet expelled sudden tension in a long, silent sigh and stepped forward into the light issuing from the office so that he could be seen. The riders reined in. Sue pushed her roan forward an extra couple of steps and gazed down at Chet.

'We rode in fast,' she said in a clipped tone. 'When Dave showed up at the Circle B with news that you had killed Floyd Carson in self-defence I sensed that your arrival had busted the whole works loose. Now perhaps we'll find out who ambushed Burt.'

'This business is really buzzing,' Decker said. 'Doc Pryce was gunned down about fifteen minutes ago. I reckon someone was trying for Chet, but it can't be Ben Carson because he won't have got word yet that Floyd is dead.'

The other riders edged their horses forward and Chet recognized Sue's elder sister, Alice, whose expression exhibited tension and worry. Alice gave no sign of acknowledging Chet, and his glance switched to the big man at her side. Sue was leaning forward in her saddle, her brown eyes narrowed as she studied Chet's face, and she glanced over her shoulder at her sister.

'You know Alice, Chet,' she observed, 'but you've never met her husband Rafe Colby, have you? He took over running Circle B when Pa was killed. And those two hardcases back there are Colby's pet dogs, Chuck Hackett and Don Farris. Did you hear about Hank, huh? He was gunned down just like Burt was. I don't see eye to eye with Rafe on a lot of things, but he's making a good job of filling Pa's boots.'

Chet frowned. Colby remained motionless, holding his big white horse in with powerful hands. He was tall in the saddle, broad-shouldered and heavily built. His face was shadowed by the brim of his

Stetson and, when he spoke, his voice was unemotional.

'So you're Burt's brother, huh? I've sure heard a lot about you, Chet. We've been wondering when you would show up. Burt always set great store by you. He reckoned you would soon get to the bottom of the trouble building up around here. But it sounds like you found a whole mess of it for yourself. I reckon if you've got any sense at all you'll spread leather and get to hell out of here before Ben Carson learns of Floyd's death.'

'I'm about to take a statement from Chet,' Decker cut in harshly. 'I'm sure you folks have got good reason for showing up here at this time of the night, but there's nothing you can do right now so why don't you all go back to Circle B and stay out of this? There's likely to be gun smoke drifting when Ben Carson does get word about Floyd.'

'We're not going anywhere,' Sue said sharply, and Chet detected dislike for

Decker in her tone. 'Dave was at Coyote Creek on my orders, keeping an eye on the Flying W while Burt is in town, and Dave saw what happened when that hell-raising bunch rode through the spread. He's given us a good report of the shooting, and he's gonna make a statement about it. Ain't that right, Dave?'

'Sure thing!' Sawtell moved uneasily in his saddle, and Chet could tell that right now the man was wishing he was a thousand miles away from this particular spot. 'Chet had just arrived at the creek when Floyd and that bunch he rides with showed up. We didn't know it was Floyd then, and it wasn't the first time a bunch of riders had come through there throwing lead into the cabin. Chet was standing at a window and a bullet smashed a pane of glass and Chet's face was cut by a flying shard. He fired in return, and his slug hit Floyd Carson.'

'You better come into the office,' Decker said harshly. 'I wanta get all this down on paper before Ben Carson shows up. Like the rest of you, I wanta know what Floyd was doing shooting up the Walker cabin out on the creek. It does sound, though, as if it was just some harmless fun that went wrong. You know how young men with guns like to fire them off. We get the same thing here in town every Saturday night.'

'So you're ready to whitewash what happened, huh?' Sawtell said harshly. 'Why don't you talk to that tough bunch Floyd rode around with? You know who they are, same as the rest of us. But it seems like everyone walks wide around them. They're always raising hell in town, and it's about time the law put a stop to them.'

'Don't try to tell me how to do my job.' Decker spoke sharply, his face twisted by a grimace. 'I got enough on my plate with the sheriff being away right now. If you think I've got an easy time of it then you should pin on a badge for a couple of days and try it out. You'd change your mind mighty quick.'

'We'll go along to the hotel and wait for you, Chet,' Sue cut in. 'I can't stand to hear a man whining about his job. Dave, tell what you saw out at Coyote Creek — nothing but the plain, unvarnished truth. We'll back you all the way in this, Chet. If Ben Carson does ride in with blood in his eye then we'll face up to him. He won't want to fight the whole Circle B outfit.'

'Sue, pull in your horns.' Colby cut in. 'It would make more sense to wait and see what happens than go off half-cocked and add to the trouble.'

'I'll play this as I see it,' Sue flashed. 'Just stick to running cows, Rafe, and I'll attend to my affairs. This concerns me, not you. And remember that I didn't ask you to ride into town with me tonight. You insisted on coming.' She glared at Sawtell. 'Dave, you do like I told you.'

'Yes, ma'am.' Sawtell dismounted meekly and wrapped his reins around the hitch rail.

Decker turned and entered the office.

Chet followed him closely. Sawtell glanced around the street before crossing the threshold, and Decker stepped aside and closed the office door with a slam.

'Sit down, both of you,' Decker directed, 'and we'll get this done before there is any disturbance.'

Chet dragged a chair before the desk and sat down. Sawtell did likewise. Decker moved around the desk and dropped into the padded seat there. He opened a drawer, produced a stack of clean white writing paper, then picked up a pen and dipped the nib into an inkwell.

'You first.' Decker glanced up at Chet. 'All I want is the plain truth with no fancy words. Start where you showed up at Coyote Creek, and keep it short.'

Chet recounted the incident and Decker's pen scratched on the paper as he wrote down the gist of what was said. When Chet lapsed into silence Decker asked him a number of questions and wrote down the answers. When he was satisfied with the statement he dipped the pen into the inkwell and handed it to Chet.

'Sign it,' he said harshly, and Chet complied.

Then it was Sawtell's turn, and Decker followed the same rigmarole, his lips silently forming the words of the statement as he wrote them down. Chet sat motionless, containing his impatience, one ear cocked for the sound of hoofs along the street. His thoughts were busy, however, flitting over the incidents which had occurred since his arrival like flies around a honeypot.

'That's all I want,' Decker said at length. 'On the face of it Floyd Carson's death was self-defence, but it ain't up to me. There will be an inquest, so the pair of you better hold yourselves ready to attend that. I'll let you know when it will take place. If you can take advice, Walker, then you will go back out to Flying W and stay there until I send for you. I reckon Ben Carson will show up here shortly, and there's likely to be gun play if he sets eyes on you. I'd like to talk to him before he goes off half-cocked, so give me a chance to smooth this out and avoid gun smoke.'

'I'll be around to talk to Ben Carson should he want to see me,' Chet replied. 'I'm not going out to Flying W. I'll be at the hotel.'

Decker opened his mouth to reply but thought better of it and remained silent. Chet got up and moved to the door with Sawtell at his elbow. They left the office, mounted their horses, and rode along the darkened street to the hotel.

'I don't like any of this, Chet,' Sawtell said as they dismounted and tied their mounts to a rail where three Circle B horses were standing hipshot. 'Sue is ready to stand up and be counted on your side, and the rest of the old crew will follow her to hell and back, but we'll be outnumbered, and the way things are going, womenfolk won't be safe if shooting starts. You should try to make Sue back down from the stand she's making.'

'Have you ever tried to get Sue to change her mind when it's been made up?' Chet countered. 'I wouldn't dream of trying, knowing her as I do. And I don't want anyone getting into this fight on my side. I don't fight like that. But it seems it is not just my fight, doesn't it? Hank Bartram was shot dead six months ago, and if he had been my father I wouldn't rest until I found the man who killed him. I guess Sue will stand up and fight to the last shot, and I'll not be the man to blame her. If she needs my help in locating Hank's killer then she'll get it.'

'This whole business is like a keg of gunpowder fitted with a slow fuse.' Sawtell paused at the door of the hotel and glanced at Chet, his expression filled with anxiety 'There's been trouble around here for a long time, simmering like a pot on a stove, but your return has lit the fuse, and now the damn thing is likely to blow up right in our faces.'

'Doc Pryce said something similar,' Chet said. 'Before we go in, Dave, tell me the names of the bunch Floyd Carson rode around with. You say it is common knowledge, but I don't know who they are so bring me up to date.'

'It ain't for me to say.' Sawtell shook his head. 'They are a few young men who got together in the first place to raise a little harmless hell, but it looks like it got out of hand and their capers worsened, especially over the last six months. I reckon you'll find out soon enough who they are. Just keep your eyes and ears open.'

Sawtell walked into the hotel and Chet followed closely. Sue was sitting at a small table in the dining room to the right of the lobby. There was no sign of Alice and Colby or the two gunmen, Hackett and Farris. Sue lifted a hand when she saw Chet and beckoned to him. He crossed to her side and she pointed to a chair opposite.

'Sit down, Chet. You and I must talk. I've got rid of Alice and Colby. Rafe is

44

against us taking your side in this trouble, and Alice isn't the same girl since she married him. Dave, we'll be staying in town tonight so you can take off, but be ready to ride at sunup. Put our horses in the livery barn.'

Relief showed on Sawtell's face and he turned instantly to depart. He paused at the street door and looked back at Chet.

'You want me to take care of your horse?' he called.

'Yeah, do that for me, Dave.' Chet sat down at the table, and moved his chair slightly to get a clear view of the street door. He looked around, marking the entrance to the dining room, and then turned his attention to Sue, who was regarding him with an intense gaze, her dark eyes glinting in the lamplight. She smiled sadly, and heaved a long sigh, then shook her head and sighed again.

'At last you're back,' she observed, 'and I'm wondering why you ever went away in the first place.'

'I'm kind of surprised you and Burt

haven't tied the knot yet,' he countered. 'What's been holding you back?'

'It was never on the cards that Burt and I would get wed. If he ever thought there was a chance for him and me then he got it badly wrong. But that's all water down the creek now. We've got this trouble on our hands, and if something isn't done to stamp it out then the whole range will burn. Rafe is for burying his head in the sand. He thinks the trouble will miss us if we don't take sides. Alice is a fool these days. Her head has been filled with other things since she married Rafe. I'm the only one who seems to know what's coming, and I've been counting the days to your return because I know you are the man to fight this. Burt wouldn't listen when I tried to warn him, and look where he is now. He's lucky to still be alive.'

'So who is behind the trouble?' Chet demanded. 'Don't say you don't have suspicions or tell me to find out myself. You must have seen this coming, and, knowing you like I do, you'll have made it your business to get to the bottom of it.'

'Sure I've got suspicions.' She shrugged. 'Pa was shot dead! Do you think I'd turn a blind eye to that? I set Dave Sawtell to checking out the ambush, but he came up with nothing. All I have to go on is that someone saw Pa come out of the bank with a wallet full of money, and killed and robbed him before he could get back to the ranch. I hounded Abe Curry for weeks, trying to get him to pull out all the stops to locate the killer, but nothing came of his efforts.'

'So Hank was robbed, huh?' Chet compressed his lips as he gazed into Sue's dark eyes. 'How much dough was he carrying?'

'He drew fifteen thousand bucks out of the bank. That much I learned from Henry Kenton, the banker.'

'That was a helluva lot of dough! What was the money for?'

'Pa was planning a trip to Texas to buy some Herefords. He wanted to start a special herd.'

'Why didn't he take a banker's draft with him instead of toting all that cash along?'

'You knew Hank!' Sue shook her head. 'He was bull-headed; said no one could rob him! He didn't expect to get ambushed on his own doorstep.'

'So someone who knew about his trip took advantage of that knowledge.'

Sue nodded vigorously. 'That's what I thought, and I worked on that angle, but it turned out the whole town knew what was going on, and there was a small crowd outside the bank when Pa went for his money. The killer could have been any one of a dozen men.'

The echoing crash of a shot out in the street blasted through the intense silence of the night. Chet sprang up instantly and made for the street door. Sue got up and he shouted at her to remain where she was. He drew his pistol as he went out to the sidewalk, and the instant he put his nose in the doorway two guns cut loose at him, tattering the night with orange gun-flame and raucous gun thunder.

3

Chet threw himself backwards out of the doorway as the shooting erupted and he heard slugs smacking into the woodwork of the building as he hit the threshold on his back. He squirmed into cover, aware that two guns were shooting at him. He stayed low while the storm of lead continued. When he threw a glance over his shoulder at Sue he saw her hunched on the floor behind the table where she had been sitting. Her face was pale in shock, but she was gripping a .38 pistol in her right hand and looked as if she was prepared to use it.

The shooting cut off suddenly. Chet sprang to his feet and cocked his pistol as he went out to the side-walk, his muscles tensed in anticipation of lead striking him. But the attackers had fled, and the darkened street seemed all the more ominous as an uneasy silence returned. He heard the sound of receding footsteps in an alley opposite the hotel but stifled an impulse to go in pursuit.

Sue came to him and grasped his arm.

'Don't go out there, Chet,' she warned. 'They might be trying to draw you into the open.'

'I doubt that,' he replied. 'I don't believe they are after me. How many folks know I'm back?'

'They were obviously watching for you to arrive at Coyote Creek. Some-one knew you were back. Everyone has been expecting you. How are you going to fight this set-up?'

'A step at a time, if I should live long enough,' he replied grimly. 'Did Burt ever mention anyone trying to buy Flying W?'

'How did you know about that?' Sue seemed surprised. 'Did Burt write and tell you?'

'No. I'm guessing. So there has been

an offer. Do you know who made it? I've got a feeling I should know that before we go any further.'

'Burt told me that Vince Sharman, the lawyer, approached him with an offer to buy your ranch from some out-of-town speculator. Burt turned the offer down, and his trouble started just after that. Do you think that unknown buyer is responsible?'

'I sure mean to find out. And how long has Sharman been operating as a lawyer in town? Dan Wilson was the lawyer when I left.'

'Wilson retired unexpectedly and Sharman bought his practice,' Sue replied.

Boots pounded the sidewalk, coming from the direction of the law office, and Chet covered the hotel doorway as the big figure of Lance Decker appeared. The deputy was holding a double-barrelled shotgun in his hands.

'What in hell was all that shooting?' Decker demanded. 'So it's you again, Walker! I might have known you would be involved. What happened this time? Have you killed anyone else?'

Chet's eyes glinted and a tingle ran through the fingers of his right hand, but he ignored the gibe.

'I didn't get the chance to fire a shot,' he replied easily. 'But my time will come. I'm wondering how anyone around here can know that I've returned. You were the only one in town who knew my identity after I rode in, so who have you told about me?'

'Me?' Decker shook his head. 'I ain't a loose-lip. I got more than enough trouble on my plate without adding to it by jawing about what's going on.'

'So what is going on?' Chet kept his tone easy but there was a hard light in his dark eyes. 'I was shot at out at Coyote Creek before I had hardly set foot on the Flying W, then there was the shooting at Doc's place, and now two guns threw a lot of lead into the front of the hotel, and I just happened to be inside. It's getting to be a bad habit around me and I want some answers pretty damn quick. If you know the names of any hardcases around here who might be interested in my return then you better spit them out and I'll look into their movements before we go any further.'

'You better not start riding roughshod around here,' Decker warned. 'The law will handle this. There's nothing much I can do tonight, but come sunup I'll be checking this out.'

'That ain't good enough, Decker,' Rafe Colby cut in, and Chet glanced around to see the man standing at the foot of the stairs with Alice Bartram behind him, looking scared. 'I agree with Chet that something has got to be done now, not in the morning. I can name half a dozen men who are probably interested in Chet's return. For a start there's that hard bunch out at Beacon Hill run by Joe Stockton. If they're not involved in this trouble then I'll eat my hat. I've warned them off Circle B range. Burt Walker said he had a run-in with Lew Pierce just before he was shot, and Pierce runs Stockton's outfit.'

'I don't know any of the names you've just mentioned,' Chet mused.

'There are a lot of newcomers in the county,' Colby said through his teeth, 'and a number of them are undesirable. But it seems the law is unable to move them on, and I reckon they are causing most of the trouble we are getting. I guess the ranchers will have to get together and run them out before it's too late to act. We're all running short on patience.'

'I don't want to hear any talk of vigilantes and lynch law,' Decker said sharply. 'I got enough trouble around here without having to fight the law-abiding people. Don't start rousing up the ranchers, Colby.'

'Then do something to put a stop to this trouble,' Colby snapped.

Decker shrugged and turned away. Chet listened to the sound of the deputy's boots rapping the sidewalk until an excited voice shouted that someone was lying dead in the street. Decker came back at a run, passing the door of the hotel. Chet moved swiftly and went out to the sidewalk He saw two men standing over a fallen figure just along the street, and a pang stabbed through him when he thought of Dave Sawtell. He noticed that all the mounts were gone from the hitch rail in front of the hotel, including his own.

Decker paused beside the two men and bent over the still figure lying in the street. The deputy stood up again almost immediately and turned to look at Chet.

'It's Dave Sawtell!' he called, 'He's dead.'

Chet walked forward, his mind frozen in shock, but deep inside him a tiny flame of anger became ignited and spread slowly through his big figure. He halted beside Decker and looked down at Dave Sawtell, noting the dark stains of blood on the man's chest. Decker was cursing softly, his face showing anger.

'This is what comes of someone sticking his nose into another's business,' Decker said fervently. 'Sawtell should not have been out at Coyote Creek. Circle B declared war by taking a hand, and whoever is running this crooked business is missing no tricks to clean up. You better take this as a warning, Walker. They're telling you that you ain't got a chance, and if you don't pull out you'll finish up on your face in the dust.'

'This is not the first time you've advised me to quit,' Chet said slowly. 'Well, I ain't a quitter, and I'll fight whoever wants to take me on.'

'Sawtell took some horses to the livery barn,' one of the townsmen said. 'He was coming back when the shooting started in front of the hotel, and a man came out of that alley over there, walked up to Sawtell, and shot him twice in the chest. It was the most cold-blooded thing I ever saw! Poor Dave never had a chance. It's pretty bad when a man can't go about his lawful business without getting shot.'

'Is Dave dead?' Sue demanded, appearing at Chet's side. She was holding her pistol in her right hand.

'He couldn't be any deader!' Decker said angrily. 'Now you can see what you'll get for poking your nose in where it doesn't belong! I tried to warn you to stay out of this, but you had to get bull-headed and jump in feet first. You've made the situation ten times worse than it might have been, and the end result will be the same as if you kept out.'

'You're talking in riddles, Decker,' Sue replied angrily. 'I'll talk to you tomorrow. Maybe I'll get some sense out of you then. Where are our horses? Have they been run off?'

'They're in the livery barn,' one of the townsmen said. 'Sawtell put them away before he was shot.'

'I'll take care of Sawtell,' Decker said. 'Let's break this up now. Jeez, it'll be dawn before I can hit the sack, and it looks like being a real heavy day tomorrow.'

Chet walked back to the hotel with Sue, and he was thoughtful. His thoughts were running swift and deep. Alice and Rafe Colby were standing in the doorway of the hotel, and Colby cursed when Sue acquainted him with the news of Sawtell's death.

'You had to get involved, and against my wishes,' he said bitterly. 'Why didn't you leave it alone, Sue? I could see what would happen but you never listen to me, do you, huh? You go against me as a matter of course, even if you know I'm right. Well, I'm getting mighty sick of trying to make friends with you. After this you can go your own way, and don't come running to me for help when you get into deep water. Circle B ain't gonna come to your rescue. If you can't be sensible about this trouble you'll have to do the other thing.'

'Don't forget I own half the ranch,' Sue retorted. 'Where do you get off telling me what I can or cannot do? You're too high and mighty, Colby. You're not married to me, and you're just running the outfit; you don't own it.'

Chet shook his head wearily. A pulse was throbbing painfully in his right temple. His thoughts were confused, and the bickering voices of Sue and her brother-in-law grated on his nerves. He needed some peace in which to gather himself mentally to face the confrontation which would surely come with the arrival of Ben Carson. He reckoned Carson would not waste any time before riding in, and if all accounts of the rancher's temperament were true then gun smoke would soon be flying.

'It sounds to me like you two have some mighty bad differences between you,' he cut in as Sue continued to attack Colby verbally. 'Why don't you take it somewhere private?' He glanced at the silent Alice, who seemed not to utter a word on either side. 'You ain't taking sides, Alice,' he observed. 'But maybe you can put a stop to this arguing. You used to have a mind of your own, so what's happened to you since you got married?'

'I keep telling her she should stand up for herself,' Sue said sharply. 'She's nothing but a doormat these days, and Rafe sure wipes his feet all over her.'

'It's no joke trying to run a ranch with a couple of ornery females in the background, questioning every order I give or trying to change whatever I say,' Colby said furiously. 'I sometimes wish I'd never seen the sky over Circle B.'

'You can quit any time you like,' Sue flashed.

Chet turned away, shaking his head. He entered the hotel. The night clerk was sitting behind the reception desk. Chet booked a room and took the key.

'I'll see you in the morning, Sue,' he said. 'I need to get some sleep.'

He left them in the lobby and ascended the stairs to his room. A sigh of relief escaped him as he entered and locked the door. He removed his cartridge belt, drew his pistol from its holster, and lay down on the bed fully clothed with the gun in his hand. But sleep evaded him while his thoughts tried to get to grips with the situation in which he found himself. Burt had certainly not overstated his problems when he wrote about the trouble he was facing at Coyote Creek.

The grey light of dawn showed against the window before Chet eventually lapsed into an uneasy slumber, and it seemed that no more than a few moments had elapsed before someone hammered on the door. Chet jerked up, his gun levelled at the door, and he sighed long and hard as he got to his feet. He crossed to the door, and was careful to stand to one side out of the line of fire should shooting erupt.

'Who is it?' he called.

'Decker,' came the hoarse reply. 'I've just had Ben Carson and half a dozen of his outfit in the law office. They're fighting mad. I told Carson you pulled out of town last night to go back to Coyote Creek, and they rode out fast. I've got you a little time, Walker, and you better make the most of it. They'll be back soon as they've checked out Flying W.'

'Thanks,' Chet replied. 'I owe you one, Decker.'

Decker's boots thudded on the stairs. Chet stood for a moment, thinking over the events that had arisen since his arrival at Coyote Creek. The knowledge of Dave Sawtell's death lay like a block of ice in his mind, and his thoughts revolved around the dead man as he prepared himself to face the new day. He checked his pistol before leaving the room, and went down to the dining-room for breakfast, unable to remember the last time he had eaten a good meal.

He was thankful that Sue, Alice and Rafe Colby were not yet down for breakfast, and hurriedly ate eggs and bacon before swallowing two cups of strong black coffee. But Sue called to him as he crossed the lobby intending to check the street for clues to the identity of the men who had shot up the hotel the night before. He waited for the girl to reach him, his eyes narrowed, hooded, his lips pinched. He was feeling prickly, but it did not show as he gazed into Sue's concerned features. She looked as if she had not closed her eyes during the night, and he made an effort to speak politely, remembering that she had stepped in to help after Burt was shot.

'Where are you going?' she demanded. 'You're not running out, are you?'

'The hell I am!' he responded, and then grinned. 'As I remember, you always did rub folks up the wrong way, didn't you? Is that why Burt never got around to marrying you?'

Shock suffused her face as his words struck home and she flushed, anger flooding into her gaze.

'I don't want to get off on the wrong foot with you, Chet,' she said hurriedly. 'I talk the way I do to Colby because I hate how he's taken over at Circle B, and his methods leave a lot to be desired. I'm against him on principle, but I want to help you, so bear with me. I've got a lot on my plate, what with Pa murdered and his killer still running around loose.'

'I'm a mite short on temper myself,' he replied. 'I've got things to do today, Sue, and I don't want you to be within a mile of me until this business has been settled.'

'You're afraid I might collect a slug that's meant for you, huh?'

'That's it. If you wanta help me go get yourself a nice breakfast, then ride back to Circle B and stay there until I can get around to calling on you.'

She gazed into his hard features for a long time, and he could see by the expression in her eyes that she was having trouble coming to terms with his attitude. Then she nodded, and a sigh escaped her. A tear appeared in her left eye and shimmered on the lower eyelashes for a moment before rolling down her cheek.

'All right, if that's the way you want it,' she said. 'See you around, Chet. Have you got any particular choice of flowers you'd like for your funeral?'

He smiled, placed a hand on her shoulder, and squeezed it gently.

'Hang in there, Sue,' he said softly. 'We'll beat this business before we're done, but it's got to be on my terms.'

He left her then and went out to the street, his right hand close to the butt of his holstered pistol. He was braced for shooting, but the bright morning was silent and still. He looked around at the familiar town, and it seemed that five years had not passed since he had last seen it. He crossed the street to the alley where the shooting had erupted the night before, and it soon became obvious that he was wasting his time looking for clues.

There was a patch of dried blood along the street where Dave Sawtell had been shot down, and Chet stood gazing at it for long moments. He moved to a sidewalk and stood with his back to a wall while his gaze took in the wide street. Folks were beginning to stir. A man in a white apron was sweeping the sidewalk in front of the general store, and a buckboard was coming into town from the range. He watched it pull up in front of the store; saw the store-keeper lean on his broom and begin chatting with the newcomer.

Chet liked the appearance of normal life, but he was aware of the dark undertones shadowing the community. There were men living here who knew what was going on, and he meant to get to them and make them pay for their villainy.

A short, middle-aged, fleshy man dressed in a light-grey store suit appeared on the opposite sidewalk and walked along with an arrogant strut that seemed to say a lot about his character. His thick shoulders swung with each step and he wore a supercilious smile on his face. He stopped outside the lawyer's office, and Chet's eyes glinted as he crossed the street to intercept the man, catching him just as the office door was unlocked and pushed open. He recalled the lawyer's name, which had been mentioned by Sue the night before.

'Vince Sharman?' Chet enquired.

'I am he.' Sharman's keen gaze swung to take in Chet's appearance, and his eyes narrowed in their fleshy sockets. Close up, Sharman looked to be in his early fifties. His face was lined, his broad forehead wrinkled, and a fine network of tiny creases surrounded his beady eyes. 'Who are you? Do we have business together?'

'I'm Chet Walker. My brother Burt was gunned down a week ago. We own Flying W on Coyote Creek.'

The change that came over Sharman was much more than imperceptible. He seemed to cringe at the mention of Flying W, and Chet, watching him intently, saw something akin to fear appear in the lawyer's dark eyes.

'So you're Chet Walker!' Sharman nodded as he struggled to regain his poise. 'I'm pleased to meet you. I have heard a great deal about you. Burt set great store in your return, but it looks as if you have arrived too late to be of any great help to him. He's been lying at death's door this past week. If you'll excuse me, I have to open my office. Good day to you.'

Sharman turned to the office door, still with the key in his hand, and stepped over the threshold. He turned to close the door and a croak of fear escaped him when he found Chet following him closely. Chet pushed Sharman against a wall.

'I got some questions to ask you, Sharman,' Chet said grimly. 'First off, who has been trying to buy Flying W? I guess the paperwork would be done by you. There isn't another lawyer within a hundred miles of Flat Ridge. So open up and tell me what is going on around here. I expect you're involved in it somewhere, so speak up or I'll be forced to beat the information out of you.'

'I know nothing of any such under-taking.' Sharman had to push his head back on his neck to look up into Chet's hard eyes.

Chet placed his right hand on Sharman's shirt-front and twisted his long fingers in the soft material. He thrust the hand upwards, his knuckles under Sharman's chin, and the little lawyer was forced to rise on his toes, his face turning a deep red as his air was cut off. He squealed like a pig about to be slaughtered, and his hands came up to flutter helplessly against Chet's powerful grip. Chet reached out with his left hand, slipped it under Sharman's coat, and grasped the belt around the man's thick waist. He exerted his strength and Sharman's feet left the floor as he was propelled up against the wall.

'I can tell you're lying,' Chet said easily. He slammed the man hard against the wall and Sharman's head made a hollow sound when it made contact. He closed his eyes and slumped in Chet's grasp. 'Come on; give with the information,' Chet continued. 'You're holding out on me, mister, but I'll get at the truth if I have to break your neck doing it.'

Sharman's eyes flickered open, filled with fear as he tried to focus his gaze on Chet's face. Chet set him back on his feet and held him against the wall.

'Are you gonna come clean?' he demanded. 'I asked you a question and I want a straight answer, so speak up before I get rough with you. Dave Sawtell was gunned down on the street last night, right outside this office. My brother was ambushed last week and Hank Bartram was killed six months ago. I want to know what's going on around here, and you'll tell me, so get on with it. I'm a mighy impatient man.'

Sharman gasped and tried to speak but only a groan passed his lips. He lifted a wavering hand to his throat and swallowed a couple of times.

'You can't treat me like this!' he gasped at length, shaking his head. 'I'll have the law on you.'

'Do you want a real roughing-up?' Chet countered, raising his hands again. 'I only asked you a simple question. Why don't you answer it?'

Sharman shrank back, his face expressing fear. 'You won't get away with this,' he declared in a rasping whisper. 'The men who are running things around here will get to you like they did your brother.'

'That's what I want.' Chet grinned. 'I'm hoping they will come for me. But I need to know who they are before they attack me, so spill the beans, mister, or I'll beat it out of you.'

'I've had dealings with the Kansas Land and Cattle Combine.' Sharman almost stuttered in his desire to impart the information. 'They have a head office in Kansas City. They've bought several properties in the county in the last six months, and put in an offer for Flying W last month. I passed the offer on to your brother but he said he had no intention of selling.'

'So then they tried strong-arm tactics, huh?' Chet demanded. 'Is that the way they run their business?'

'No, no!' Sharman protested. 'You've

got it wrong. They are not that kind of an outfit. They are quite reputable. As I said, they've bought other properties in the county and there was no trouble.'

'Who has sold out to the Combine?' Chet insisted.

'Nick Latham comes to mind, and Frank Kett. They pulled out with no trouble at all. Now you'd better leave. I shall talk to the sheriff when I see him, and he'll have something to say about the way you've acted. You can't go around like a mad bull.'

'I can,' Chet replied. 'Someone else is doing just that, but I'll take a hand in this business now, and we'll see a different outcome, I promise you. I'll be back to see you again if I find you're holding out on me in any way.'

Sharman staggered when Chet released him, and Chet stepped out to the side-walk, his gaze instinctively covering the street. More folks were moving around now, and he saw two men coming along the sidewalk towards him. Something in their manner seemed to suggest they had business with him, for they both dropped their hands to the butts of their holstered pistols when they saw him, and one half-turned his head to speak sharply to the other.

Chet paused, his right hand down at his side, the butt of his gun pressed against the inside of his wrist as he prepared for trouble. The pair halted three yards away from him.

'I'm guessing you're Chet Walker,' one said.

'That's right.' Chet nodded. 'What's it to you?'

Neither man replied, but both reached for their pistols, their action setting Chet into motion. He drew his Colt fast, and the next instant the early morning silence of the town was shattered by the quick blast of gun fire.

4

Chet's pistol cleared leather and lifted smoothly, his thumb cocking the weapon before it left his holster. The man on the right was faster than his companion by a fraction, and Chet fired when the blade of his foresight lined up on the man's chest. As the shot crashed out he swung his gun to the left and beat the second man to the shot. He fired and the bullet took the man in the centre of the chest even as his companion released his hold on his gun and fell to the sidewalk.

Chet stood with narrowed gaze fixed on the hapless pair. The second man twisted and flopped down to join his companion on the ground. Chet moved forward and kicked their guns into the dust of the street. He glanced around as echoes faded. Those people going about their business were momentarily frozen in shock, and all heads were turned in the direction of the disturbance. Chet heard a movement at his back and his head jerked around. He saw Sharman peering out of the office doorway with stark fear on his pasty features.

'Who are these two?' Chet demanded, and Sharman shook his head frenziedly, too shocked to find his voice. 'They knew me,' Chet continued. 'Are they strangers in town?'

Again Sharman shook his head. He backed away and slammed his office door. Chet grimaced. He looked along the street and saw Lance Decker coming at a half-run from the law office. Sue Bartram was emerging from the hotel, and she let Decker pass before following swiftly. Decker was breathing heavily when he halted in front of Chet, shock stamped indelibly on his coarse features. He had drawn his pistol, but now thrust it back into its holster.

'What in hell happened here?' Decker demanded, his voice trembling, 'I might have guessed you'd be involved, Walker.'

'They asked if I was Chet Walker, and when I said I was they both drew their guns. I shot them in self-defence.'

'Who are they?' Decker looked at the two sprawled figures without going close to examine them.

'Don't you know?' Chet countered. 'I haven't been around here in five years, but you live here. You should know them.'

'I ain't seen either of them before.' Decker shook his head. 'What in hell are two strangers doing, riding in here to shoot you? They must have followed you from Montana. I don't think they have anything to do with the trouble around here.'

'How can you be sure?' Chet shook his head. 'Where the hell has Abe Curry gone? We could do with him being here right now.'

'I told you, the sheriff is away on a trip.' Decker shrugged his thick shoulders.

'Where has he gone? A sheriff worth his salt wouldn't leave the county for personal business with the kind of trouble he's got around here.'

'That's his business, not mine.' Decker turned his attention to the converging townsfolk attracted by the shooting. 'Joe, go fetch Milner. Tell him there are two stiffs down here to be removed. I'll see him later.'

A townsman turned and hurried away. Decker moved to the corpses and dropped to one knee beside the nearest. He searched the man's pockets but found nothing of significance and turned his attention to the second man, with the same negative result.

'They ain't carrying anything to say who they are,' he grumbled. 'I'll check with the livery barn to see when they rode in. I'll need a statement from you about this, Walker. I wish you had left town like I suggested last night.'

'It's just as well I didn't go back to Flying W,' Chet observed.

'I sent Ben Carson out there because I knew you were in town. But you better watch your step because he'll be back here when he finds Flying W deserted.'

Sue arrived, breathing hard. Her dark eyes were wide in shock, her face pale.

'Are you all right, Chet?' she demanded.

He nodded, realized he was still holding his pistol and returned it to its holster with a slick movement.

'Did you kill both those men?' Sue gazed at the bodies in horror.

'If I hadn't killed them they would have killed me,' Chet responded. 'Have you seen them around town before, Sue?'

'No, but I saw them out at Circle B about a week ago.' She shook her head. 'They rode in looking for jobs. I didn't cotton to them, but Rafe considered taking them on until Alice put her foot down. It was about the only time she's come down on my side of the fence since she married that skunk.'

'Did Colby take them on?' Decker demanded. 'Stick to the point, Sue. I ain't interested in your fights with your brother-in-law.'

'He didn't give them work,' Sue said hesitantly. 'He fed them and then escorted them off the spread. I thought they would have been long gone by now. I wonder why they stuck around. Were they waiting for you to show up from Montana, Chet?'

Alice and Colby came along the sidewalk and paused to gaze silently at the two dead men.

'They're the men who showed up at the ranch last week,' Sue said sharply to Colby. 'Did you hire them, Rafe? I know you always do the opposite to what I say.'

'The hell I did!' Colby replied testily. 'What would I do with a couple of lazy drifters? I could tell what they were the minute I clapped eyes on them.'

He grasped Alice by the arm and began pulling her away.

'I want to visit the store before we return to the ranch,' Sue said. 'Have the horses saddled and bring them along the street, Rafe.'

'You fetch your own damned horse,'

Colby replied. 'I ain't your servant. When you learn to treat me with some respect I'll start looking after your interests.'

The sound of hoofs along the street caught their attention and Chet turned to see who was approaching. Sue uttered a frightened gasp when she saw three riders approaching at a canter.

'Be careful, Chet,' she warned. 'That's Ben Carson and two of his riders, and by the look of Carson's face he ain't in the mind to just talk.' She dropped a hand to the .38 Colt pistol stuck in the waistband of her pants. 'You're not alone in this,' she vowed grimly. 'Carson better not try anything.'

Chet reached out and took the gun from her hand.

'Stay out of this,' he said sharply. 'Get along to the store now, if that's where you have to go.'

'Are you loco?' she demanded. 'My father was killed six months ago, and I've always suspected Ben Carson being back of it.'

'Now you tell me.' Chet eyes narrowed as he watched the approach of the three riders. 'Was there any trouble between Hank and Ben Carson?'

'Enough to make me think Carson shot Pa, or paid someone to handle the chore.' Sue replied harshly. 'Give me my gun and I'll make a stand right here.'

Chet shook his head. The three riders reined in to the sidewalk and halted their mounts. The foremost man was big, middle-aged, of powerful build with a hard face and unblinking brown eyes which looked like a couple of polished stones from a creek bottom. He was dressed in a dark-blue store suit and wore a black JB pulled low on his forehead to shade his gaze. The two men with him were hardcases, well-armed and intent, their concerted gaze fixed on Chet as if they had already decided he was their target.

'What happened here?' Carson demanded, gazing at the two dead men. 'Who killed them?'

'Ben, I asked you to stay away from town for a spell,' Decker said desperately.

'You must be loco if you think I would ignore Floyd's death. I wanta see the man who killed him.' Carson's hard gaze rested on Chet's big figure. 'Are you Chet Walker?' he demanded. 'You got the look of Burt Walker about you.'

'I'm Chet Walker,' Chet agreed. 'Can you tell me why your son Floyd would ride through Flying W throwing lead?'

'He did that?' Carson made an involuntary move of his right hand to the butt of his holstered pistol but halted the action before it was completed.

'He was with several other hellions.' Chet spoke firmly. He explained what had occurred, and Carson shook his head doubtfully.

'So you shot him down like a dog, huh?'

'He came close to puffing a slug through my head,' Chet replied. 'I'm real sorry I had to kill him. I would have preferred talking to him — to find out why he was raiding the Flying W, but there was no chance.'

'Where's Floyd's body?' Carson shifted his attention to Decker.

'I took him along to Milner's place, Ben. I'll go along there with you.'

'Why did you send me out to Flying W knowing Walker wouldn't be there, huh?' Carson began easing his hand towards the butt of his gun. 'You gave me the run-around, Decker, and I don't like it.'

'I was just doing my job.' Decker spoke obstinately.

Carson's gaze flickered back to Chet. 'I got things to do right now,' he said. 'I'll look you up again later. If you told the truth about what happened out at your place then I guess I got no cause to shoot you.'

'Who was Floyd riding around with?' Chet demanded. 'You should be looking them up, and I'd like to ask them a few questions.'

'I'll get around to them in due

course.' Carson twitched his reins and his horse turned away obediently.

Chet watched the man ride off back along the street in the direction of the undertaker's establishment. He heard Decker heave a sigh of relief. Sue plucked at Chet's sleeve.

'Don't trust Carson, Chet,' she said firmly.

'What makes you think he might have had something to do with Hank's death?' Chet countered.

'There was some trouble last year over water rights. Carson rode into Circle B claiming the right to use our stream for his cattle and Pa chased him off the spread. The next thing we knew, Pa was dead, and Carson rode around for a long time looking like the cat that got the cream.'

'What has the law done about it?' Chet turned to Decker, who shook his head.

'You'll need to talk to the sheriff when he gets back. I got to go along the street and talk some more to Ben

Carson. Don't let us have any more shooting, huh?'

'Sure.' Chet nodded. 'The next time someone wants to shoot holes in me I'll let him do it, huh?'

'That ain't what I mean and you know it.' Decker's face flushed and he turned away angrily, his boot heels thudding on the wooden sidewalk as he departed.

'You've changed some since I saw you last, Chet,' Sue observed. 'Now you're prickly as a cactus. What have they been feeding you on in Montana?'

'I was all right until I got Burt's message.' Chet gazed around the street. 'At first I thought he was exaggerating, but the minute I showed up at Flying W I became a target, and I've been knee-deep in trouble ever since. I find the sheriff is away on a trip, and Decker ain't talking about what he knows of the situation. Doc Pryce got himself shot last night simply because he was at my side when I was leaving his house. Burt was gunned down last week, and you hit me with the news that your Pa was shot and killed six months ago, and nothing has been done about it.'

'We did a lot about it.' Sue spoke in a rasping tone. 'We nearly turned the county upside down, but there was nothing to point guilt in any direction. I have my own ideas about it, of course, but there's nothing I can do without some kind of proof.'

'I know what you mean. So what's the trouble between you and Rafe Colby? You two are like a cat and a dog locked together in a barn.'

'I didn't like him taking over running Circle B.' Sue grimaced. 'He married Alice, moved in, and before I knew what was happening he had hold of the reins of the ranch and I was forced to stand to one side and watch him. I don't like him, Chet. He's hired some mean gunnies, although they keep us free of trouble. But he was a gambler at the Red Dog saloon before he latched on to Alice, and he's been rubbing me up the wrong way ever since he took over the ranch.'

'It sounds like he's doing a good job.' Chet heaved a sigh. 'I'd better get along to the docs place and check on how Burt is doing this morning.'

'I'll come with you.' Sue spoke eagerly. 'I need to see Burt for myself. I've only seen him once since he was shot. I'll walk to the doc's with you.'

'The hell you will!' He shook his head firmly. 'It's mighty dangerous even to stand by me right now. You get back to Circle B and stay there until I got time to come calling. Bear in mind that your pa was murdered and the killer might be planning to clean up on the rest of your family.'

Sue looked startled and a flash of fear showed momentarily in her eyes. Then she held out her hand.

'Give me my gun,' she urged. 'I'm never without it these days.'

He handed over the weapon and Sue stuck it into the waistband of her pants.

'I'll be looking for you to ride out to

Circle B on a visit.' she said.

'It won't be for some time because I've got to get back into the swing of things around here. I need to follow up a few points that have cropped up since last night, and I reckon I'll be kept pretty busy for a few days.'

'Don't take any chances,' she said in a flat tone.

Chet smiled and turned away. He walked along the sidewalk to Doc Pryce's house and knocked on the door, which was opened by Bill Newton, the horse doctor. Newton's long face was grim, and he sighed with relief when he recognized Chet.

'Say, am I glad to see you?' he said. 'Doc is giving me hell about handling him like a sick horse. He's overlooked the fact that treating animals is my job, and he doesn't appreciate the fact that I dug the slug out of him last night. But it's your brother I'm really worried about. He needs a lot of nursing, and I'm out of my depth where he is concerned. Doc's wife died last year or she would have taken over here, so I don't know how you're gonna handle this. I don't think Burt can be moved yet, so you'll need to bring in someone capable of nursing him.'

'Is Doc sitting up and taking notice?' Chet demanded. 'I'll need to have words with him.'

'He sure is, and that's the trouble.' Newton grimaced. 'He's giving me a dog's life with his orders and advice. I never got a wink of sleep all night.'

Newton led the way into the doctor's office and Chet found Doc Pryce lying on the examination couch with a blanket over him. His right shoulder was heavily bandaged and shock showed plainly on his lined features.

'Chet, I'm glad to see you,' Pryce declared. 'I'm being treated like a sick mule. Bill doesn't know the first thing about caring for people.'

'You're more mule than man,' Bill Newton responded, shaking his head.

'You look pretty good for a man who took a slug last night, Doc,' Chet observed. 'Is there anyone in town we can get in to take care of you and Burt?'

'Mrs Clarke usually helps me out when I need a nurse. Maybe you'll go ask her to drop by and see me.' Pryce stifled a groan as he eased himself up on the couch. 'Burt is gonna need a whole lot of nursing before he gets out of the wood. Don't try to move him out of here, Chet.'

'Can I go up and see him?' Chet asked.

'Sure thing!' Pryce nodded. 'The sight of you right now will do him better than anything I could give him. Don't stay too long though, and don't let him talk too much.'

Chet nodded and turned away eagerly. He ascended the stairs to the bedroom where Burt was lying and walked in on his brother. Burt seemed to be asleep, and Chet moved to the side of the bed and gazed down at his pallid features.

'Burt,' he called gently. 'Are you awake?'

Burt's eyes flickered but did not open, and Chet called his name again. Burt opened his eyes, peered up at Chet and, recognizing his visitor, tried to speak but no words came from his throat. He lifted his right hand weakly and held it out. Chet grinned and shook hands, finding no real strength in the limb, and sat down on the side of the bed.

'How are you feeling now, Burt? Doc told me you've had a real bad time of it. Have you got any idea who shot you?'

Burt made another attempt to speak but could manage nothing better than a croak. He turned his head slightly and looked towards the small bedside table — nodded at a jug of water standing there. Chet half-filled a glass and held it to his brother's lips. Burt took several sips and then sighed heavily.

'Chet,' he said in a hoarse whisper. 'Thank God you're here at last. I've been counting the days. But you better be real careful. Someone has declared an open season on Flying W.'

'Have you got any idea who shot you?' Chet repeated.

Burt shook his head. He slumped a little, as if his few words had exhausted his frail strength. Chet tried another angle.

'You wrote me saying you'd got trouble at the ranch,' he said. 'What was that all about?'

A shadow crossed Burt's face. He shook his head slowly. 'There's bad trouble,' he said hoarsely. 'Don't let them get behind you, Chet.'

'Who are they?' Chet asked patiently. 'You must have some idea who was giving you trouble. Can you give me any names?'

Burt sighed again and closed his eyes. Chet gazed at his brother's impassive features, noting beads of sweat of Burt's forehead and sunken cheeks. There was a grey pallor in Burt's face which looked most unhealthy, and anger stabbed through Chet at the sight of such a big, healthy young man prostrated by an ambusher's slug. He patted

Burt's shoulder.

'Just take it easy, Burt,' he said softly. 'You concentrate on getting better. I'll take care of the trouble now. It won't take me long to get into the swing of things. You're on the mend, so keep making progress, huh?'

Burt nodded slowly but did not open his eyes. He began to breathe deeply, and Chet realized that his brother had fallen asleep. He shook his head sorrowfully and left the bedroom to go back to the doc's office. Bill Newton was standing just inside the doorway, a grin of relief on his weathered face, and Chet saw a middle-aged, buxom woman bending fussily over Doc Pryce.

'Mrs Clarke is taking over here,' Newton said, and the woman turned quickly to look Chet up and down.

'I hope you haven't been upsetting your brother,' she declared. 'He needs complete rest and lots of nursing.'

'I think he was glad to see me,' Chet replied. 'I'm here to help him, not hinder his progress.'

'From what Doc tells me, Burt will need nursing around the clock,' Mrs Clarke observed. 'I can handle the nights because I'm widowed, and my daughter will stand in for me each day. She's well accustomed to nursing. I taught her well.'

'Thanks.' Chet nodded. 'I'm beholden to you, Mrs Clarke. I'll pay whatever it costs to get Burt back on his feet.'

He departed then, and stood on the sidewalk looking around the street while his thoughts turned over the events which had taken place since his arrival. He saw Alice and Rafe Colby emerge from the hotel and mount their horses to ride off at a canter, and wondered what Sue was doing. There was certainly no love lost between Sue and her brother-in-law, but then Chet did not like the ex-gambler. He remembered the man from the days before he left Flat Ridge, and distrusted anyone who lived by his wits on the fringe of lawlessness. Gambling was a devious profession, and in his experience most gamblers were crooked in one way or another.

He saw Ben Carson walking along the opposite sidewalk from the under-taker's parlour, and spotted the two gunnies Carson had ridden in with making for the stable, one of them leading Carson's horse. It looked like the C7 rancher planned to stick around for a spell, and Chet wondered which way the man would jump when his emotions finally got the better of him. He reckoned Carson would be gunning for him, although he had killed Floyd in self-defence.

Vince Sharman appeared on the doorstep of his office as Carson passed, and the lawyer spoke to the rancher, who halted in mid-stride and replied to Sharman's greeting. Chet watched them talking, and would have given a lot to have heard the gist of what was being said. He realized he would have to confront Sharman again to find out more about the Kansas Land and Cattle Combine. Someone was causing the trouble in the county, and usually a person trying to buy into the community was the perpetrator.

Chet moved on along the street, making for the Red Dog saloon. If the bartender there didn't know what was going on around town then no one would know. He passed the lawyer's office on the opposite side of the street, and kept an eye on Ben Carson as he moved on to the Red Dog. When he pushed through the batwings and entered the saloon he strode to the nearest corner of the polished bar. Then he wondered if he had made a mistake, for a tough-looking gunman was bellied up to the bar, drinking beer and talking loudly to several men standing around him.

The gunman fell silent at Chet's entrance. The bartender, a stranger to Chet, was short and fleshy and wearing an off-white apron. His sparse black hair was slicked down with too much grease. He came along the bar to serve Chet.

'What'll it be?' the 'tender demanded.

'Beer,' Chet replied. 'Jim Dent used

to be the bartender here. What happened to him?'

'He left years ago.' The bartender grimaced, and subjected Chet to an intent gaze. 'It must be some long time since you were last in here, mister. Charlie Cooper used to own this establishment, but he sold out to Frank Telford, and I took over Jim Dent's job. I'm Bill Twitchett.'

'Chet Walker,' Chet responded. 'I'm back after five years away, and it seems the whole county has upped and pulled out and strangers have moved in.'

'They call it progress.' Twitchett slid a tall glass of beer in front of Chet.

'There never used to be any trouble, as I remember,' Chet observed. 'So what's gone wrong? There's been shooting all over the place, and dead men were lying in the street earlier.'

'I heard the shooting,' Twitchett agreed, 'and there has been some killing over the past six months, but it's the same all over the West. Like I said, they call it progress.'

Chet paid for his drink and Twitchett moved away along the bar. Two of the few customers finished their drinks and departed hurriedly, casting glances at Chet as they left. Chet ran his gaze over the remainder, and did not see one face he knew from before. He noted that the gunman was watching him intently, and wondered at his interest. It was clear that no one was talking about the current situation, and Chet sensed that fear was the reason for the silence.

He drank from his glass, using his left hand and, as he swallowed, his gaze remained on the gunman. He saw the man's right shoulder lift slightly and sensed that he was drawing his holstered gun. Chet reached for his own weapon instantly and it came to hand easily. The gunman thrust his pistol at an angle over the top of the bar. Chet saw the muzzle gaping in his direction and started shooting. The next instant the saloon reverberated to the hammering blasts of gun fire.

5

A slug tore into the bar top a scant inch from Chet's left hip as he squeezed his trigger. His gun blasted and the gunman spun around and fell to the floor, kicking spasmodically. The stench of burned gunpowder stung Chet's nostrils as he looked around for more trouble, but the four men remaining at the bar were motionless, faces pinched in shock, their hands in view on the bar top. The 'tender's mouth was agape in silent protest, his eyes wide and glittering as he gazed at Chet's grim figure.

Chet swallowed to clear his ears of gun thunder. He walked around the bar to stand over the fallen gunman, who was stretched out on his left side, gun discarded in the sawdust. A patch of bright blood stained the man's shirt-front in the region of his heart. Chet heaved a long, silent sigh and shook his head. He shifted his gaze to the bartender.

'Who is this guy?' he demanded.

'I never saw him before,' the 'tender replied shakily. 'He walked in here about ten minutes ago, bought a beer, and never said a word about his intentions. He began asking questions about what was going on around here, but most strangers do that.'

Chet holstered his gun, his fingers steady. He had expected to walk into trouble upon his return home but not to this extent. He realized that he had to get his investigation moving before one of these gunnies got lucky and plugged him. He turned swiftly as the batwings were thrust open, his pistol appearing in his hand, ready for action. Lance Decker appeared, breathing heavily, and halted swiftly at the sight of Chet's grim figure and levelled gun.

'It's you again!' Decker observed bleakly. 'So what happened this time?'

Chet stood silent while the bartender

explained. Decker shook his head, his face troubled.

'He's a stranger to me,' he said, looking down at the dead gunnie. 'Where did he come from? All these hardcases are coming into town like flies gathering round a honeypot. Who's put out the word there's trouble here?'

'I'm bothered by the same question,' Chet observed. 'It's getting so I can't turn around without falling over someone planning to shoot me.'

'I told you to get out of town until I can find out what is going on,' Decker grumbled.

'That would give them, whoever they are, a better chance to finish me off.' Chet shook his head. 'I'm gonna stay right here until I get some leads on who is causing this trouble, and perhaps you'd better stick close to me and watch my back, Decker. It's the only way you're gonna get anything done.'

'I'm running the law single-handed.' Decker shook his head. 'I sure wish the sheriff was here.'

Voices were talking loudly outside the batwings, and Chet saw townsmen gathering, attracted by the shooting.

'Why don't you pull out until I get this sorted?' Decker pleaded. 'There was no real trouble around here until you showed up last night.'

Chet opened his mouth to make a cutting remark but a burst of gunfire on the street changed his mind and he ran to the batwings as echoes rippled across the town. The men outside the saloon were scattering. Chet hit the sidewalk fast, his gun lifting for action. He saw a buckboard loaded high with bits and pieces of furniture coming along the street, its team running in fright, its driver slumped in his seat. Someone ran out, grasped the bridle of the nearest horse, and halted the wagon.

A dozen men crowded around the buckboard and willing hands lifted the driver from his seat and stretched him out in the dust.

'It's Caleb Jones!' someone said.

Chet frowned. He knew the name.

Jones worked a small ranch north of Coyote Creek. He pushed his way through the crowd, aware that Decker was at his side. One glance was sufficient to show him that Jones was dead.

'Did anyone see what happened?' Decker asked. 'Who did the shooting?'

'A couple of riders caught up with the wagon just as it turned into the street,' someone said. 'I looked around at the first shot and saw the riders shoot Jones before hightailing it back out of town.'

'Did you recognize them?' Decker persisted.

No one answered, and Chet heard the deputy mutter a curse.

'Johnson, go saddle my horse, and half a dozen of you better ride along with me. We'll hunt down those two killers. Will you side me, Chet?'

'No.' Chet shook his head. 'I need to get a line on the trouble Jones was getting. It sure didn't start right here on the street. Why was he driving a buckboard full of his furniture? It looks like he was running from something which caught up with him right here.'

Decker bent over the crumpled figure and searched its pockets. He shook his head when he discovered nothing of any significance, and looked around at the tense faces watching him.

'Does anyone know what was going on with Jones?' he demanded. 'Parker, you knew him well! When did you last see him?'

'He was in town a couple of days ago,' Parker replied, shaking his head. 'I had a few words with him. He wasn't too happy. He said he had to see Sharman, the lawyer, about some business that had come up. He went into Sharman's office, and that was the last I saw of him.'

'I'll go with you, Decker, if you want to talk to Sharman,' Chet said instantly. 'I reckon he's got some questions to answer.'

'I need to get after the two men who killed Jones.' Decker shook his head.

'I'll talk to Sharman later.'

Chet turned away and eased out of the crowd. He saw Sharman standing in front of his office and walked in that direction. Sharman spotted him, turned instantly, and hurried into his office. Chet quickened his pace and pounded along the sidewalk. When he reached the door of the lawyer's office he found it locked. He hammered upon it.

'Open up, Sharman,' he called, 'or I'll break down the door.'

There was no reply and Chet peered through the window into the office. There was no sign of the lawyer. A door in the back wall stood ajar. Chet ran to the adjacent alley and sprinted along it to the back lot, reaching the rear of the building in time to see Sharman running into the alley beside the bank. He followed instantly, turned into the same alley, and saw Sharman disappearing out of the street end.

This was more like it, he thought as he followed. Sharman was acting suspiciously — he was certainly fleeing, and Chet intended getting a reason for Sharman's fright.

A big, tough-looking man was standing at the entrance to the bank. He was wearing a brown store suit and a brown derby. His face looked as if a bad-tempered mule had knocked him down and taken its time to kick him repeatedly. His nose had been broken and badly set and his dark eyes peered out suspiciously from puffy, bruised skin which had never recovered from the hammering it had evidently received in countless fist fights. He had the build and power of a stockyard bull, and looked just as bad-tempered.

'Hey, hold it right there,' the big man exclaimed when Chet approached him. 'What is your all-fired hurry, mister?'

'I saw Sharman come in here and I need to talk to him,' Chet replied. 'Who in hell are you?'

'Matt Lawson. I guard the bank. Mr Sharman did just come in, and told me to keep you out. What's your business?'

'You'd better stay out of this,' Chet

said patiently. 'Stick with your duties, Lawson. You don't take your orders from Sharman.'

'It's my job to see that bank customers don't get bothered when they are attending to their business.' Lawson's right hand slid with practised ease inside the lapel of his jacket. 'You better wait outside or you just might get hurt, mister, and we don't want that kind of trouble, do we?'

Chet drew his pistol with a fluid movement, the weapon appearing in his hand so unexpectedly that Lawson fell back a pace in surprise before he halted and gazed down at the muzzle of the weapon jabbing him in the stomach. A spark of fear showed momentarily in his dark eyes and his mouth gaped as Chet reached out with his left hand for the snub-nosed revolver in the shoulder holster under the brown jacket.

'You can have this back later,' Chet said. 'Just back off and stand quiet over by the far wall.' He glanced around the inside of the bank, looking for the lawyer. 'Where is Sharman?' he demanded.

'He went into Mr Kenton's office,' Lawson mumbled, backing off.

Chet crossed the floor, opened a door in the back wall, and peered into the banker's office. A big man in shirtsleeves was seated at a desk but there was no sign of Sharman.

'Did Vince Sharman come in here?' Chet demanded.

'No, he didn't.' Henry Kenton looked up. 'What do you want? You can't come bursting in here. If you want to see me you'll have to make an appointment.'

'Are you Kenton?'

'I am. Who are you and what is your business?'

'Lawson told me Sharman came in here, so where is he?' Chet moved to a door in the rear wall of the office and jerked it open. He stepped out to the back lot and looked around, his eyes narrowing when he saw Sharman astride a grey horse, riding hell for leather from a barn twenty yards away.

Chet looked back at Kenton, who was sitting motionless at his desk, both hands in view, his fleshy features pale and eyes bright with fear.

'Who owns that barn out back?' Chet demanded.

'It belongs to the bank,' Kenton replied.

'And the grey horse Sharman is riding?'

'That's mine. Sharman has borrowed it.'

'I thought you said Sharman didn't come in here.'

'I protect my business associates where I can.' Kenton shrugged, his grey eyes narrowed.

'So Sharman burst in here a few moments ago, demanded to borrow your horse, and then ducked out. Didn't that seem suspicious behaviour to you?'

'It wasn't quite like that.' Kenton shook his head.

'So what was it like? You better speak up because Sharman is getting away and I need to talk to him urgently.'

'He came in and told me he was being chased by a gunman. I told him my horse was in the barn out back and he dashed out. Why are you chasing him?'

'That is my business, and I'll be back later to talk to you, Kenton. How long have you been in charge here? Dan McCarthy used to run this bank.'

'I've been here three years. I took over from McCarthy when he retired.'

'I'll talk to you some more when I get back with Sharman,' Chet promised. 'I need to know who is buying up ranches in the county.'

'You won't get that information from me,' Kenton said smoothly. 'That is private bank business.'

'I think you will be pleased to tell me what you know when I've got the time to ask questions,' Chet promised.

Chet departed by the back door and went along to the livery barn. He saddled his horse, rode across the back lots to the barn behind the bank, and dismounted to check the fresh hoof-prints in the thick dust. He found the spot where he had seen Sharman riding away, and noted the deep, wide prints of the grey where it had set off at a gallop. He looked towards the rear of the bank and saw Kenton and the guard, Lawson, standing at the back door watching him. He swung back into his saddle and set off at a canter to follow Sharman's tracks.

At last he had something to work on. Sharman must have lost his nerve after their confrontation earlier, and Chet wondered where the lawyer was going. He had certainly wasted no time quitting town, and seemed to be riding north. Flat Ridge dropped behind, and Chet had an easy task tracking his quarry across the undulating range.

He wondered where Sharman was heading, and wished he knew more about the lawyer. He remained alert as he rode, aware that a desperate man just might drop behind a skyline with a weapon and shoot to kill from ambush.

He pushed on faster, intent upon getting within sight of his quarry.

Sharman's tracks eventually veered left and reached a trail leading off to the west. Chet frowned when he realized the lawyer was riding in the general direction of Circle B. He considered Rafe Colby and did not like what he recalled of the ex-gambler. Colby had married well but did not get along with his sister-in-law. Generally Sue was easy enough to rub along with, but the girl obviously resented Colby's intrusion into Circle B life after her father was killed.

He saw other fresh prints on the trail and recalled that he had seen Colby and Alice riding out of town earlier. Was Sharman intent on getting to Circle B? Chet decided to play a waiting game. He could take Sharman any time he wished, but if the lawyer led him to others who had a hand in the trouble then so much the better. He ascended a slope, reined in just below the skyline to check the trail ahead, and ducked back quickly when he saw three figures in the middle distance, huddled together in a serious conversation.

Chet recognized all three immediately. Rafe Colby and Alice were talking with Sharman, and the lawyer was waving his arms and shaking his head. Colby was leaning forward in his saddle, waggling a forefinger under Sharman's nose. Chet dismounted, trailed his reins, and then bellied up to the crest to observe. He removed his hat and gazed with interest at the scene ahead. He was still watching intently when he heard the sound of a horse approaching from his rear.

Chet rolled back from the crest and gained his feet in a lithe movement, his pistol coming to hand like a well-trained tool. The approaching rider reined in and gazed at him. Chet lowered his gun, frowning as he recognized Sue Bartram.

'What the devil are you doing here, Sue?' he demanded.

'I was about to ask you the same

question.' She rode closer. 'I have to come this way to get home, remember. What is your excuse for acting so suspiciously? Who is over that ridge? What are you up to, Chet? I thought you were still in town. What has brought you out here?'

He explained tersely and saw amazement appear on Sue's expressive face. She dismounted quickly and almost ran up the slope to look over the crest, but Chet grasped her arm and pulled her back.

'They might spot you,' he warned. 'I want Sharman. He knows something about the trouble we're getting. I braced him earlier and he seemed like a man with a guilty conscience. What can you tell me about him?'

'Not much. I've never had any dealings with him, but Colby has.' A trace of bitterness sounded in Sue's voice. 'In fact that's where the trouble between Colby and me started. Sharman turned up at Circle B one day and said he had a client who was interested in buying Circle B range up around Beacon Hill. He mentioned some big business combine who wanted to run cattle up that way.'

'Was it the Kansas Land and Cattle Combine?' Chet prompted.

'That's right.' Sue looked surprised. 'How'd you know about that? Did Burt write you?'

'No. I heard it mentioned this morning. So what happened? Did Colby sell that range through Sharman?'

'We had a big row about it. I was against the sale but Colby wanted to sell, and things have stayed bad between us ever since. I was against selling because Pa used to say that land was power, and he was always ready to buy any range which came up for sale. But Pa was killed before Sharman showed up with his offer, and it is likely that Colby sold that land even though I was against it.'

'It sounds like your pa was killed to get him out of the way.' Chet let his thoughts roam over the situation. 'Was

Alice agreeable to selling that range?'

'She wasn't against the idea. Anything Colby wants to do is OK by Alice. He's turned her head completely. I think she'd agree to run sheep if Colby wanted to.'

'So did Burt ever discuss his troubles with you?' Chet eased forward to peer over the crest and saw Sharman in the act of swinging his mount away from Colby, who reached out and grasped the lawyer's reins to detain him.

'Burt never talked about his problems.' Sue eased up beside Chet and studied the trio in the middle distance. 'I wish he had. But you know your brother even better than I do. He's always been close-mouthed. I saw him become a very worried man, and he had good reason to be, the way he was shot down just like Pa. Do you think Colby is mixed up in this crookedness? I've never liked the way he's acted since taking over Circle B.'

'I don't know anything yet, but I mean to find out,' Chet declared.

'Shall I ride down there and try to find out what is going on?' Sue suggested. 'They'll be expecting me to ride back to the ranch this morning. You stay back out of sight, and follow us from cover if you need to. I'd like to know what is going on between Sharman and Colby. It looks like Colby doesn't like Sharman's presence at all.'

'I hesitate to agree to you riding into danger.' Chet shook his head. 'If Colby is back of this trouble then your life wouldn't be worth a plugged nickel. I want you to stay out of it, Sue. I can handle this now I've got some leads to follow.'

Sue eased back from the crest, got up and ran to her mount. She swung into the saddle and kicked the horse forward over the crest, avoiding Chet's out-stretched hand as he made a grab for her reins. The next instant she was over the crest and riding hell for leather down the slope. Chet dropped back into cover and lay with teeth clenched as he watched her rapid progress.

Sharman was trying to pull his reins free of Colby's grasp when Sue reached the group. Chet watched intently. Sue reined in and asked a question. Colby shook his head and released Sharman's reins. He reached out then, snatched the .38 pistol from Sue's waistband, and stuck the muzzle under the girl's nose.

Chet caught his breath as he stifled an impulse to confront Colby. He could tell by the attitudes of Sue and Colby that a big argument had developed. Alice sat motionless on her horse, just watching, and she seemed to be in another world for all the reaction she showed. Sharman swung his horse and attempted to ride away but Colby grasped the lawyer's reins with his left hand and a tussle ensued which ended when Colby swiped Sharman with the barrel of Sue's .38. Sharman fell sideways out of his saddle and slumped motionless on the hard trail.

Sue launched herself at Colby, who struck her shrewdly with his left fist.

The blow stunned Sue and she almost slid from her saddle, but she swung her horse around and set off at a gallop towards the distant Circle B. Chet saw Colby lift the .38 and aim at Sue's back, but Alice became animated and spurred forward to grasp Colby's gun wrist. Colby struck his wife with a back-handed blow that dazed her. He looked in Sue's direction but the girl was fast disappearing over a nearby ridge and he turned his attention to the fallen lawyer.

Sharman was stirring. Colby dismounted, grasped the lawyer by the shoulders and hauled him to his feet. He thrust the muzzle of the .38 under Sharman's nose and the lawyer dropped to his knees, his face contorted in fright. Chet remained watching although his instinct was to reveal his presence and put a stop to Colby's bullying. For some moments it looked as if Colby would shoot Sharman, but he eventually lowered the pistol and slapped Sharman's upturned face several times with an open palm. He stepped back then and waved his left hand as he shouted at the lawyer. Sharman got to his feet, staggered to his horse and mounted, then rode away rapidly, huddled in his saddle.

Chet crouched motionless as Colby swung into his saddle and took off at a canter in the direction of Circle B. Neither he nor Sharman looked back at each other as they parted, and Chet sat back on his heels as he considered what he had witnessed. He had no idea what was going on, but the actions of Colby and Sharman gave him a hope that watching both men in future might present him with some idea of what was happening in the county and who was behind it.

The sound of a gun being cocked at his back brought Chet's attention back to his surroundings and he whirled quickly to see Matt Lawson, the bank guard from Flat Ridge, standing motionless with a levelled rifle in his hands and a big, leering smile on his battered face.

'I got you dead to rights,' Lawson

snarled, 'and I have orders to put you out of it, mister, so get your hands up and I'll draw your fangs. You've just come to the end of your trail.'

6

Chet gazed at Lawson through narrowed eyes as the man approached to disarm him. He was poised to overpower the man should the opportunity arise, but Lawson evidently knew what he was doing for he took no chances. He closed in on Chet from behind and whipped the pistol out of Chet's holster.

'That's better.' Lawson grinned. 'Now let us find some nice quiet spot where I can bury you.'

'Who gave you orders to kill me?' Chet demanded.

Lawson swung his left fist in a tight arc and his heavy knuckles crashed against Chet's jaw with the force of a runaway train. Chet ducked instinctively but could not avoid the blow, and the impact of the fist caused a black curtain to slip down over his sight. He was dimly aware of falling over backwards. His shoulders hit the ground and his senses whirled. He remained motionless, waiting for his senses to stop gyrating, and heard Lawson's voice, seemingly remote, urging him to get up.

Chet opened his eyes as the effects of the blow diminished to find Lawson standing over him, pointing the rifle at his head.

'That's better, mister. Come back to me. It was only a little tap I gave you. Wait until I really hit you! Up on your feet now! We got to get moving.'

Chet rolled off his back and pushed himself to his hands and knees. He paused to wait for his senses to stop whirling and Lawson kicked him in the ribs.

'You're wasting time, mister,' Lawson rasped. 'Come on, get up. I've got to get back to town when I've settled you, so don't hang around. Let us get this done quick.'

Chet pushed himself upright and

stood swaying, his eyes half-closed, his chin on his chest, but he was watching the big man, intent upon taking any chance to get the upper hand. But Lawson did not make any mistake. He stayed out of reach and the black eye of his rifle did not waver as he covered Chet.

'Who are you working for?' Chet repeated. 'Who sent you out here to get me? Was it Kenton? Is he mixed up in this trouble? I heard the bank was raided last year. Who did that, huh?'

'You sure can ask a helluva lot of questions, mister.' Lawson slid his left foot forward and his left fist travelled about six inches in a deadly arc to Chet's chin, but Chet was ready this time and leaned backwards slightly from the waist, allowing the heavy knuckles to skim by their target. His left hand shot out and secured a hold on Lawson's rifle. He twisted the weapon aside and sledged his right fist against Lawson's chin.

The move took Lawson by surprise

but the blow did not appear to inconvenience him at all. Lawson half-twisted away, trying to drag his rifle hand from Chet's grasp, and when that failed he threw himself over backwards, taking Chet with him. They landed heavily on the ground and Chet concentrated on keeping hold of Lawson's gun. Lawson squirmed and arched his back, throwing Chet off, and Chet lost his hold on the rifle.

Chet twisted and rose to his feet, found Lawson swinging the weapon in his direction, and lunged forward, aiming a kick at Lawson's rising hand. His dusty toe caught the fingers clenched around the butt of the rifle and the weapon flew out of Lawson's grasp. The big man jerked up on his feet, both hands extended in front of his fast-moving body. Chet could not avoid the rush but managed to half-turn away as he slid his right arm under Lawson's left armpit. He ducked and twisted, and Lawson flew through the air before landing on his head. He cried out in shock and relaxed instantly.

The bank guard lay motionless on his face. Dust rose from the ground in little spurts as he gasped heavily through his gaping mouth. Chet picked up a discarded gun, found it was his own, and covered Lawson as he moved in. He stayed out of reach of the man's dangerous hands, but Lawson was out cold.

Chet shook his head to clear it and his sense of balance gyrated. He dropped to his hands and knees as the world swung and tilted before his eyes. The tumult eased and he arose, staggered to his horse, and took a pair of handcuffs from a saddlebag. Lawson was still motionless when Chet snapped the cuffs around his prisoner's thick wrists.

Gazing down at Lawson, Chet was pleased with the turn of events. He looked around but the range was deserted as far as he could see. He looked in the direction Sharman had taken and knew he had to get after the lawyer. Thinking of the violent scene he had witnessed between Colby, Alice and Sue, he had to fight an impulse to head straight for Circle B and deal with Colby.

Lawson began to stir and Chet stood over him with levelled gun. Lawson's eyes flickered open and he gazed skywards for some moments, until awareness filtered into his eyes. He shook his head and tried to raise a hand to his face. The handcuffs clinked and he reared up and gazed in shock at his hands.

'Say, what is going on?' he demanded.

'I got some questions that need answers pretty quick,' Chet told him. 'If you don't go along with that I'll take you back to Flat Ridge, throw you in a cell and lose the key.'

'Are you another of those undercover lawmen, mister? There was one in Flat Ridge not long ago, sneaking around and asking questions.' Lawson grinned harshly. 'They soon laid him to rest.'

'I'll ask the questions; you concentrate on truthful answers.'

'You wanta do a deal, is that it?'

'I wouldn't trust you if you were dead,' Chet told him.

'I'll tell you what you wanta know if you'll turn me loose afterwards and let me ride out of the county,' Lawson said eagerly.

'No dice! Murder has been committed. I'm gonna hold you until I get the killers and the men who have been causing the trouble around here. Let's try some general questions before we go any further, huh? Who shot my brother Burt last week?'

Lawson shook his head. 'Why ask me? I hang around the bank six days a week. I don't know anything about your brother.'

'What about Hank Bartram's murder six months ago?'

'Likewise, I don't know a thing about that. I was shocked when I heard what happened.' Lawson grinned as he spoke.

'Wipe that grin off your face or I'll remove it with the barrel of my gun,'

Chet rasped. 'So you're a real hard man, huh? OK. You can sweat a little. I reckon you'll come round to my way of thinking before we're through. Get on your feet and mount up. We're gonna make tracks.'

Lawson lumbered to his feet under the menace of Chet's pistol and climbed into his saddle. Chet swung into leather and took hold of Lawson's reins. The big man made no comment as they set out at a canter. Chet picked up Sharman's trail and travelled fast, determined to force a breakthrough despite his scanty knowledge.

Sharman had headed north again, away from Circle B, and Chet considered the range ahead, wondering where the lawyer was going. Ben Carson's C7 ranch lay to the north along with several smaller spreads, and Chet's eyes narrowed as he considered the dangers of showing himself around the Carson place. He kept a close watch on the now sullen Lawson as they continued.

When Sharman's tracks veered slightly,

Chet realized the lawyer was making for Coyote Creek. He sat up a little straighter in his saddle and sharpened his alertness when Flying W appeared, the sun glittering on the smooth water of the creek. There was an air of desertion around the little cow-spread as Chet reined up in cover but he caught a glimpse of a figure walking across the yard and hurriedly dismounted.

He drew his pistol, dragged Lawson from his saddle and pushed him to the ground, to bind his feet together with a short length of rope which he carried on his saddle horn. Lawson remained silent while Chet looped an end of the rope up through the handcuffs and back to the ankles and tied Lawson's wrists to his ankles.

'Don't go away while I'm checking out the spread,' Chet said with a tight grin, and Lawson cursed him bitterly as Chet moved away, gun in hand.

Knowing the area intimately, Chet angled through cover until he was looking down into the front yard. His eyes glinted when he saw three horses, two without saddles, standing in front of the big cabin his father had built many years before. Three men were standing in front of the cabin, and one of them, Chet saw instantly, was Vince Sharman. The lawyer was talking seriously to the other two and waving a hand to emphasize a point.

Chet studied the two men confronting the lawyer and decided they were strangers. He wondered what they were doing on the ranch, for they looked as if they had moved in. A wisp of smoke was drifting through the bright air from the chimney of the cabin, and one of the men turned abruptly and disappeared inside the building, to reappear in the doorway several moments later wiping his hands on a dish cloth. He spoke to his companion, who stepped aside from facing Sharman and motioned with a hand for the lawyer to enter the cabin. Sharman seemed to be on friendly terms with the men, Chet noted.

Sharman entered the cabin without

demur and the two men followed him closely. Chet looked around. There was no sign of others about the place and he eased to his right, found cover, and started to circle the cabin, wanting to get in close in the hope of picking up an inkling of the situation. He gained the rear of the building and sneaked in against the wall, where there was a small window beside the rear door.

Chet removed his hat and craned sideways to take a quick glance through the dusty window. He could hear the murmur of voices but they were not loud enough for him to understand what was being said. He saw Sharman seated at the table with one of the men while the third man was dishing up a meal that had been cooking on the stove.

Easing back from the cabin, Chet checked his pistol before moving slowly around the cabin to the open front door. His gun was in his hand, cocked and ready for action, when he stepped in through the doorway. The sound of his boots on the wooden floor attracted the attention of the three men. Sharman looked up and froze into immobility at the sight of Chet's ominous figure. The two strangers looked round quickly as Sharman fell silent in mid-sentence. One of them started to his feet and reached for his holstered gun. The other sat motionless, gazing at Chet in shock.

'Hold it! Pull that gun and you'll die,' Chet said sharply. 'Sit down and keep your hands in view.'

Sharman immediately placed both hands on the table. The man who had risen paused and remained motionless for a few dragging seconds while he contemplated what to do. Chet could see indecision in his eyes, but common sense prevailed, for the muzzle of Chet's steady gun was covering him. He raised his hands and sat down.

'What are you doing here, Sharman?' Chet demanded.

The lawyer shook his head wordlessly, apparently too shocked to speak.

Chet regarded Sharman for a few moments before turning his attention to the strangers.

'Who are you two?' he asked. 'It looks to me like you've moved in and made yourselves at home.'

'I'm Tom Coe and he's Will Rackham.' Coe was tall and thin; his angular face alive with tension, his mean eyes narrowed, watching for a chance to resist. 'We ride for C7. Ben Carson left us here in the night to watch for the riders who were with Floyd when he was killed. So who are you, mister?'

'He's Chet Walker,' Sharman cut in tensely, finding his voice with an effort.

'The man who killed Floyd?' asked Rackham, and his fleshy face grew taut.

'Yes — Burt Walker's brother,' Sharman added quickly.

'So Ben Carson left you here, huh?' Chet mused. 'Well, I don't need your help to find those riders who came in here with Floyd. You two can get out right now, and tell Ben Carson I'll do my own hunting.'

Both men started to their feet.

'Hold it.' Chet ordered, and they froze, their expressions tightening. 'Get rid of your pistols, one at a time, and don't make any fast movements because I'm hair-triggered. You do it first, Coe.'

Coe lifted his pistol from its holster, using forefinger and thumb only, and dropped the weapon to the floor. Rackham followed suit and Chet motioned to the open door. Both men departed quickly. Chet moved into the doorway and watched them saddle their mounts.

'Dump your rifles on the ground,' Chet ordered tersely, and the men complied reluctantly.

Chet remained motionless until Coe and Rackham had ridden clear of the yard. He watched them head west in the direction of C7 before returning his attention to Sharman.

The lawyer had sat motionless throughout, his sweating face expressing great fear. He cringed in his seat when Chet moved to his side.

'What were you saying to Rafe Colby earlier?' Chet demanded.

Sharman shook his head emphatically. 'I haven't seen Colby in several days.'

'You lie every time you open your mouth,' Chet observed. 'I guess that's a natural thing for a lawyer to do, but you better level with me now or you'll be in real bad trouble. I saw you meet Colby on the trail earlier and there was quite a discussion between you two; so what gives?'

Sharman licked his lips nervously. He was breathing heavily, as if he had been running. His eyes held a hunted expression, and he glanced around as if seeking some means of escape.

'You're really scared!' Chet said. 'So tell me about it. Get it off your chest. I don't know how deeply you're involved in this trouble but you sure as hell are guilty of something, and I mean to get it out of you before we ride back to town. Spill the beans, Sharman. There are two ways you can handle this, and the easy way is to tell the truth. The hard way is to keep quiet, in which case I'll have to beat a confession out of you. For me the end result will be the same so I don't care which attitude you take. You'll talk all right. But if you are stupid enough to try and hold out you'll be in a God-awful mess by the time I lock you in jail back in Flat Ridge.'

Sharman shook his head. His eyes were filled with abject fear.

'You got it wrong,' he gasped. 'I'm just a county lawyer going about my business. You scared me badly in town this morning. I'm not a fighting man and I hate violence, so when you bullied me I lost my nerve. Then you killed those two gunmen who braced you outside my office and I thought you would kill me next!'

'You ran when I came to talk to you after Caleb Jones was killed on his wagon!' Chet accused, his tone deliberately harsh. 'You ducked out the back door of your office, ran to the bank, told Matt Lawson to stall me, and high-tailed it out of town on Kenton's horse. That wasn't fear, Sharman; it was plain, old-fashioned guilt. So let's get down to cases. Why did you run from me back in town?'

Sharman shook his head. He swallowed nervously and beads of sweat showed on his forehead.

'When I caught up with you I saw you talking to Rafe Colby on the trail,' Chet continued. 'It looked like he was bullying you into returning to town. He knocked you off your horse, and when he turned on Alice you took off again and rode here. So you better start explaining what you were doing before I lose my patience.'

Sharman seemed to shrink in his seat. He was shaking his head desperately, as if trying to forget a bad dream. Chet remained silent for several moments, hoping the lawyer would crack and begin talking. The silence deepened and Sharman gave no indication of revealing what he knew.

'You mentioned the Kansas Land and Cattle Combine.' Chet tried another angle, and Sharman flinched as if he had been struck physically. 'Tell me who in the county have sold their property to that combine.'

'I can't remember off-hand. I'd need to look up the files in my office back in town.'

'Quit stalling.' Chet heaved a sigh. 'I'm fast losing my patience, Sharman.'

'I tell you I don't know a thing about what's going on! I didn't want to get mixed up in this in the first place. They told me it would be easy work. I didn't know men were going to be killed, and when that happened it was too late for me to back out.'

'Keep talking,' Chet encouraged. 'You're doing all right now, but give me some names. If you do that I'll turn you loose. You can ride out of the county if you wish, and keep going. I won't stop you.'

Sharman quailed as if he were being lashed with a bullwhip. He closed his eyes and shook his head.

'You might let me go but they wouldn't permit me to get away if I blew the whistle on them. They're playing for high stakes, and they are merciless. I'm as much a victim of their crookedness as the men they have killed.'

'Why did Kenton loan you his horse to get away from me?' Chet persisted. 'That isn't the act of an honest banker. You were mixed up in land grabbing because of your position in the county, and I reckon Kenton is in it, providing money or foreclosing on mortgages. Who are you two working for? Is it the Kansas Land and Cattle Combine? Is that how it is worked? If Kenton is mixed up in it then that would explain why Matt Lawson rode out of town after me. He got the drop on me and was intent on killing me.'

'Lawson followed you out of town?' Sharman straightened in his seat and glanced around fearfully. 'He must be after me!' he gasped. 'Kenton would have ordered him to kill me because I lost my nerve. Where is Lawson now? He's a Combine man, sent in to push through any local deals.'

'Take it easy,' Chet said soothingly. 'Lawson is out of it now. I got the better of him and he's under arrest. He's wearing handcuffs, and will see the inside of the jail as soon as we get back to town. Now start giving me the rest of it. I want it straight from the start. How did you get mixed up with the Combine, and who else is working for them? Who shot my brother last week and who killed Hank Bartram six months ago? There's a lot you can get off your chest, Sharman. What about the bank robbery last year and the stagecoach robbery? Come on; get to talking now you've started. There's no way back. You've got to keep talking. It's your only way out of this mess. Tell me everything and you just might clear yourself.'

Sharman was gasping for breath, terrified by what he had started and aware that he was caught in a cleft stick.

'You'll have to protect me from them!' he gasped, his face the colour of a whitewashed wall. His hands were trembling uncontrollably.

'You're safe for the moment,' Chet encouraged. 'Spit it out, Sharman. The sooner you do that the sooner you'll get out of here.'

Sharman gazed at Chet for a long moment, his mouth agape, his chest heaving. He swallowed noisily. Chet had never seen anyone so scared in his years as a deputy sheriff. He reached out with his left hand and slapped Sharman's face lightly, causing him to jerk upright. Sharman groaned in fear and nodded his head.

'OK!' he gasped. 'I'll tell you everything. Give me some water and I'll talk.'

Chet turned away to get Sharman a drink and at that moment a pistol hammered deafeningly, filling the cabin with thunder. Chet swung towards the door, his gun coming to hand. He saw Matt Lawson standing in the doorway, still handcuffed but with a smoking .45 in his right hand which was pointing at Vince Sharman. Lawson was grinning, his brutal face twisted with grim pleasure. He swung the pistol in Chet's direction even as Chet cocked his deadly gun, and the next instant the cabin was rocked by the blasting roar of two levelled guns.

7

Chet hurled himself sideways to the floor as his foresight lined up on Lawson's powerful body. He fired swiftly, dimly aware that Lawson was already shooting, and felt the bank guard's first shot slash across the outside of his left bicep like a lightning flash that burned with the intensity of a branding-iron. Lawson dropped to one knee as Chet's bullet struck him in the lower right rib, but the shot did not impair his action. His muzzle shifted a fraction, following Chet's rapid movement as he hit the floor on his left shoulder and rolled to his left, endeavouring to keep one step ahead of the shooting.

Lawson fired again and a sliver of wood sprang out of the floor a scant inch from Chet's right hip. Chet fired a second shot, his foresight wavering in

Lawson's direction, but his aim steadied as the gun lined up on Lawson's chest and dust spurted from Lawson's brown jacket. The gun spilled quickly from his hand. For a split second Lawson froze, and then his mouth gaped and his eyes closed. A red splotch of blood appeared in the centre of his chest and he slumped to the floor as the life drained out of him.

Chet lunged to his feet, wondering how Lawson had freed himself from his bonds and managed to get his hand on a gun. He heard a noise outside the cabin and swung to face the door as a figure appeared in the doorway. Chet recognized Coe, one of Ben Carson's men. Coe was holding a rifle which he had picked up in the yard. He swung the long gun into action but Chet was ahead of him by a fraction of a second. Chet's pistol hammered and Coe took a half-inch slug of lead in his stomach, the impact of the strike hurling him backwards out of the doorway.

A shout sounded outside and Chet

dashed to the door and peered out to see Rackham cocking a rifle and preparing to fight. Coe was lying on his back, dead or unconscious. Rackham fired hastily and his shot struck the front wall of the cabin a foot to Chet's right. Chet sent a slug at Rackham which toppled him into the dust, then he stood with pistol upraised, waiting for further resistance. Gun echoes faded slowly across the illimitable Kansan prairie.

Chet heaved a long sigh to rid his lungs of cloying gun smoke. His ears were ringing from the shooting and he forced a yawn in an attempt to clear them. He stepped out of the cabin and kicked the discarded rifle out of Coe's reach, then did the same to Rackham. When he checked the two C7 riders he found Coe probably breathing his last and Rackham already dead.

Full silence returned and Chet holstered his pistol and went back into the cabin. He bent over Lawson, found the man was dead, and turned his attention to Sharman. His teeth clicked together when he saw the lawyer sprawled dead on the floor with a stream of blood oozing from a wound in the right side of his chest. He eyed Lawson, who had made a fatal mistake in shooting Sharman before attempting to deal with Chet.

So Sharman was out of it now! Chet was disappointed. He had been on the point of getting information from the lawyer when Lawson intervened. Wondering how Lawson had managed to get free, Chet went outside and dropped to one knee beside Coe, whose eyes were flickering although he seemed to be unconscious.

'Can you hear me, Coe?' Chet said loudly. 'Come on, open your eyes and look at me.'

Coe emitted a groan. His eyes flickered open but were unable to focus. They rolled slightly and Chet suppressed a sigh, for Coe looked too far gone to be of any use, but he persisted, calling Coe's name insistently. At last

Coe managed to focus his gaze; he looked up into Chet's grim face. His mouth opened and he muttered something which Chet could not understand. Chet bent lower over the stricken man.

'Take it easy, Coe,' he said. 'You're in a bad way. Did you turn Lawson loose?'

Coe nodded. Blood dribbled from his nose and mouth and an ominous rattling sounded harshly in his throat as he drew breath.

'I heard your horse whinny as we left the yard,' he said slowly. 'We circled around and found Lawson tied and turned him loose. Lawson had a pistol in his saddlebag so we came back with him to get you. Carson told us to stay here no matter what, so we had to fight.'

'Is Carson mixed up in the trouble?' Chet demanded, and then fell silent as Coe relaxed into death.

Chet got to his feet and looked around, his ears still ringing from the effects of the shooting. He checked the wound he had taken and discovered that he was bleeding profusely from a bullet slash. He removed his neckerchief and tied it tightly around his bicep, then reloaded the spent chambers of his pistol.

His thoughts flickered back over the grim incident and he realized that despite his efforts his knowledge had barely increased. All he knew was that Lawson worked for the Kansas Combine and he had reason to suspect that Kenton, the banker, was involved with Sharman in the crookedness. The presence of Coe and Rackham pointed to Ben Carson being interested in whatever was going on.

Chet dragged Sharman's body out of the cabin and put it in the yard, then arranged Lawson, Coe and Rackham beside the inert lawyer, intending to collect the mounts of the dead men and convey them to Flat Ridge. He was crossing the yard to fetch his own mount when he heard hoofs approaching and swung around to see a rider cantering towards the ranch. He halted and stood awaiting the newcomer's arrival, his right hand resting lightly on the butt of his holstered gun.

Lance Decker rode into the yard. The deputy was grim-faced, his narrowed eyes glinting under the brim of his Stetson. He reined up in front of the cabin with the nose of his horse almost touching Chet's face and sat motionless for several dragging seconds while he stared down at the four dead men. Chet waited patiently, not moving, but ready to pull his gun if Decker showed signs of hostility.

Decker heaved a sigh, stepped down from his saddle and trailed his reins. He looked around the spread before turning his gaze on Chet.

'I thought I heard shooting from way back,' he said. 'What in hell happened here? What's Sharman doing out here, for God's sake? Why did you kill him?'

'I didn't kill Sharman!' Chet recounted the grim incidents that had occurred and saw a range of emotions flit across

Decker's fleshy face from pure shock to arrant disbelief.

'You're telling me Lawson was working for some out-of-town business organization that's forcing ranchers off their spreads so they can buy them on the cheap? Is that what this trouble is all about?'

'That's about the weight of it,' Chet agreed.

'So where do you come into this?' Decker shook his head. 'You've killed half a dozen men today.'

'All in self-defence,' Chet pointed out.

'That's as maybe, but how did you get involved? You're up to your neck in it.'

'Sure I am! I'm part owner of this spread. My brother was shot last week and when I turned up those men involved in the crookedness had to try and kill me.'

'And you think Kenton the banker is involved in this crooked business?'

'I guess he is according to how he

acted when Sharman ran away from me in town earlier. I chased Sharman into the bank and learned that Kenton told Sharman to get out of town, and lent him a horse to do so. I trailed Sharman out here, and Lawson caught up with me on the trail. He got the drop on me and said he was gonna kill me.'

'But you got the better of him.' Decker shook his head. 'I don't know what to make of all this. I sure as hell wish the sheriff was back from his trip. Can you imagine the trouble I'm gonna have trying to explain what happened when I take these bodies back to town for an inquest?'

'What are you doing here anyway?' Chet asked. 'How come you rode out here at this time?'

'I got word of you riding out of town hell for leather so I came looking for you. I never saw a man get into so much trouble in such a short time. I'm out of my depth in this business. I was all right doing the job while the sheriff was around giving the orders, but there's too much going on for one man to handle.' Decker shook his head, his expression grim. 'I've been in touch with the marshal in Kansas City, asking for another deputy to be sent down here, but so far I ain't had a reply.'

Chet grimaced as he considered. It seemed the situation needed bolstering, and he was the only man in a position to administer the necessary shot in the arm of the local law. He had been pondering the situation regarding Decker, wondering if the deputy was honest or mixed up in the crookedness, and this seemed like a good time to find out. He reached into his breast pocket for his deputy marshal badge and held it out for Decker's inspection.

'Marshal Hicks sent me in under cover to check on what's happening this way,' he said as Decker's eyes widened. 'The previous deputy was killed so I'm playing it real careful. Keep this strictly between the two of us, Decker, and we just might be able to get to the bottom of what's going on. We'll have to play our cards close to the vest to make any headway.'

'I guessed you had to be more than you said.' Decker's observant eyes glinted. 'Are you gonna step into the sheriff's boots while he's away? I could sure do with some help running the law.'

'I've had some experience in law dealing,' Chet replied. 'I was a deputy sheriff in Montana for three years, but I don't want to get involved with your office. I have to work alone, but I'll lead this investigation if you feel you can't handle it. I'm short of good local knowledge, so if you can shed some light on what is happening around here I'd appreciate it. I've got my own suspicions already, and I've only just taken a hand in the game, but you've been around a long time, and you must have some ideas on who might be caught up in this business.'

'Who do you suspect? Give me their names and I'll tell you if I agree with you.'

'Kenton sent Lawson out after me when I chased Sharman,' Chet mused. 'I shall be very interested to hear what Kenton has to say when we get back to town. Sharman told me Lawson was working under cover for the Kansas Land and Cattle Combine, so I have a lead back to them but I'd like to talk to any rancher who has sold out recently.'

'Lawson was friendly with Joe Stockton, who runs the Big S ranch over to Beacon Hill. They were as thick as thieves, and maybe that is exactly what they were. Stockton doesn't look like a man who came up the hard way. If he is running Big S for that Combine then we ought to put some pressure on him.'

Chet nodded. 'OK. Let's get over to Beacon Hill and have a talk with Stockton. We'll come back for these bodies later and take them to town.'

'I'm gonna enjoy this,' Decker said. 'It's about time I had something positive to do. The sheriff sure picked a bad time to make his trip.'

'Where has he gone?' Chet asked.

'He's got a brother in Colorado whose health is bad, so he's gone to visit with him. He took a month's holiday, and he's been gone two weeks. I'll sure be glad to see him back, I can tell you.'

They prepared to ride out. Chet fetched his horse in from where he had hobbled it and gave the animal a drink at the creek. He checked his pistol and then stepped up into the saddle. Decker was ready and waiting and they rode out, leaving the ranch silent and four bodies stiffening in the strong sunlight.

It was an eight-mile ride to Beacon Hill and Chet used the time to question Decker further about the local situation, but it was evident that the deputy had little or no knowledge of what was really going on in the county.

'Can you name the men Floyd Carson rode with?' Chet persisted. 'Who did he hang around with when he came into town?'

'Danny Stockton was Floyd's side-kick,' Decker said after some reflection.

'We'll maybe see him at Big S because he's Joe Stockton's son. They were hell-raisers, and folks walked wide around them when they'd been drinking, which was often. There are half a dozen youngsters who don't work regular and are always on the prod. I thought they were just growing up tough, but now it looks like they could have been getting into real trouble on the side. Kenton's son, Owen, is another who hung around with Floyd, and seemed to be the ring leader.'

Chet nodded, mentally agreeing that they were getting on the track of the troublemakers. He quickened the pace, intent on making contact with Joe and Danny Stockton; impatient now to follow up his leads.

Beacon Hill was a solitary stretch of high ground rising up out of the range, and the Big S ranch nestled in the shadow of this unusual prominence, consisting of a good frame house beside a meandering stream, two barns with a low bunkhouse to the rear and a corral off to the right. A neat rail fence surrounded the yard and the spread looked like it was well run.

Chet reined in and eyed the place for some moments while Decker sat his mount patiently, waiting for Chet to take the lead. There was some activity around the big yard and Chet dropped a hand to his pistol.

'Some of those men in the yard are carrying rifles,' Chet observed, 'and it looks like some of the windows in the house are broken.'

'You're right.' Decker squinted from under the pulled-down brim of his Stetson, 'and there are a couple of corpses lying on the porch.'

Chet looked at the porch and saw two sprawled figures there. He touched spurs to his horse and sent the animal forward into the yard, sitting straight in his saddle, his right hand resting on his right thigh in close proximity to the butt of his deadly Colt. Several men around the yard began to close in on the porch as they rode in, and drawn weapons were pointed in their direction.

'That's Lew Pierce, the ranch foreman, standing in the doorway of the house,' Decker informed Chet. 'I wonder what's been going on here!'

'We'll find out shortly,' Chet replied.

Pierce was well past his youth, a tall, powerful man with greying hair and a hard face almost black from years of riding the range under a blistering sun. He stood on the porch beside the two dead men, a Winchester in his hands, the muzzle of which pointed at Chet's tall figure. Three men carrying rifles reached the porch and stood motionless, their weapons held ready for action.

'What brings you out of town, Decker?' Pierce called hoarsely. 'Did you smell gun smoke?'

'Looks like you've had some real bad trouble,' Decker replied. 'What happened here? Who's dead?'

'A bunch of riders came in about an hour ago, shooting up the place. The boss was downed right where he was standing, and Danny was killed when he ran out of the house to check on his pa. Those killers sat out here shooting at everyone and everything in sight before they rode off, and they left before we could grab our weapons. I sent a couple of men to track them but they haven't come back yet.'

'Did you recognize any of them?' Decker asked.

Pierce shook his head. 'They were wearing neckerchiefs up over their faces, and I ducked into cover until they were riding out; there was too much lead flying around to take any chances.'

'Was anyone else hit?' Chet asked.

Pierce eyed him intently before shaking his head. 'I got a feeling I ought to know you,' he said, frowning. 'Your face looks kind of familiar, mister.'

'I'm Chet Walker. My brother Burt runs the Flying W. Was anyone else hit during the shooting?'

'Nope. It looked like that bunch was after Joe and Danny and pulled out soon as they went down.'

'Did any of your crew return fire?' Chet persisted. 'Were any of the raiders hit?'

Pierce shook his head. 'I got no reports on that.'

'Have you any idea where the raiders came from?' Decker asked. He was sweating profusely, and dragged a cuff across his forehead.

'No one saw them riding in. The first we knew they were milling around in the yard and shooting, and they rode out fast afterwards. You'll find their tracks outside the gate. There were six of them and they stayed close together in a bunch as they headed west.'

Chet left Decker talking to Pierce and led his horse across the yard to the gate, his keen eyes searching the ground for tracks. Once clear of the yard he became even more intent, and found the fresh tracks of six horses heading off at a gallop into the west. Two other sets of tracks showed slightly to the right of those left by the raiders, and Chet nodded approvingly.

Decker came to his side. 'Looks like they could be easy to follow,' the deputy said, 'but I ain't much of a hand at trailing.'

'I'll follow them.' Chet turned slowly and looked back at the ranch house. Pierce was standing motionless on the porch, badly shocked by the deaths of Joe and Danny Stockton. 'Does anything strike you as odd about the shooting here?' he asked.

Decker shook his head, his expression blank. 'You tell me,' he said.

'We think Floyd Carson is mixed up in the trouble because I dropped him out of that bunch raiding Flying W. You said Danny Stockton hung around with Floyd, and if the same bunch which hit Flying W came in here this morning then why was Danny shot?'

Decker looked mystified for a moment before his expression cleared. 'I see what you're getting at,' he said at length. 'The bunch that came in here shooting wasn't the same bunch that hit Flying W because they wouldn't have shot one of their own men — Danny Stockton. But there could be another angle. Perhaps they were after Danny. He might have gone against the bunch after Floyd was killed. Ain't that likely?'

'That's a thought.' Chet grimaced. 'I guess the only way we'll get at the truth is by running that bunch to ground and learning what they have to say about it. I'll take out after them. You better go back to Flying W and take those four bodies into town. I'll come on to Flat Ridge when I've handled this chore.'

'Sure thing! I hope you catch up with those killers. I'll get Pierce to take Joe and Danny into town.'

Chet swung into his saddle and rode out, keeping to one side of the tracks as he followed. He rode fast, reading the prints easily, and remained alert as he crossed the undulating range. There were two of the Big S crew ahead of him and they were unaware of his presence. He needed to catch up with them before he did anything else.

The tracks were easy to follow and Chet pushed on faster. He knew the country intimately, and wondered where the raiders were heading. He felt optimistic now, with a definite lead to follow, and rode confidently, intent on catching up with the raiders. He covered several miles before hearing the distant sounds of shooting, and reined in on the slope of a ridge to dismount, snatch his Winchester from its scabbard and belly down on the sun-baked ground to crawl forward and look over the crest.

Gun smoke was drifting across the middle distance. Chet narrowed his eyes and took in the scene below his position. Several rifles were firing from the opposite slope at a small cluster of rocks situated in the low ground between the ridges. Only one weapon was returning fire from the rocks, where a horse was down, apparently dead, and another was grazing some yards away from the scanty cover.

Chet frowned. It looked as if the two Big S men had ridden into an ambush and ducked into the rocks. He saw two figures sneaking towards the rocks from the high ground opposite, and even as he spotted them one threw up his arms and fell upon his face as a bullet from the rocks struck him. The shooting from the high ground increased furiously. Chet counted five weapons in action against the one man holed up in the rocks.

Chet pulled back, returned to his horse and set out to circle behind the attackers. Shooting continued sporadically as he rode under cover. He moved to the right, found a draw and used it to ascend the opposite slope. When he rode out of the draw near the top of the ridge he saw six horses hobbled in a picket line. Gun smoke was drifting fast from the ridge. He dismounted, hefted his rifle in his hands, and moved in the direction of the shooting.

He approached the six grazing horses from behind, ready for trouble in case one of the raiders was watching the animals. He needed to check the animals for brands, and had almost reached the nearest horse when a man arose from cover off to his left at a distance of twenty yards and fired a pistol at him without warning. Chet felt a stunning blow in his left thigh and hurled himself sideways into cover, landing heavily. His head struck a rock and he was plunged instantly into a blackness which engulfed him in silence and unconsciousness.

8

Chet regained his senses to find himself lying on his back. He opened his eyes and gazed up at the brilliant sky, unable, for several moments, to recall what had occurred. He was surrounded by a heavy silence, and felt no inclination to move until pain assailed him and stabbing shafts of agony lanced through his left thigh. He stifled a groan and lifted a hand to his head, which was throbbing painfully. His hat had fallen off and his fingers encountered dried blood on his right temple.

He made an effort to shatter the inertia which gripped him and rolled on to his right side. When he pushed himself into a sitting position the ground seemed to tilt and roll in sickening undulations. He sat with his head in his hands until the movement eased, and then raised his head gingerly and opened his eyes to look around.

The silence was complete. The six horses had gone but his black was grazing some yards away. He spotted his rifle lying to his left and eased towards the weapon, picked it up and checked it. The movement caused his leg wound to bleed and he examined his left thigh to find a bullet gouge in the flesh four inches above the knee. He tore a strip from his shirt-tail and used it to bind the wound.

He pushed himself to his feet and swayed as he looked around. The rifle was held ready to continue the fight as he limped painfully along the ridge, looking for the raiders, but they had gone. When he reached a spot from which he could look down at the huddle of rocks where the two Big S men had been in cover he saw both of them sprawled lifeless on the hard ground.

Chet turned to where the six horses had been picketed and saw their tracks heading out to the south-east, the prints wide apart and fairly deep, indicating that they were moving at a gallop. It looked as if the raiders were now heading for Flat Ridge. He turned back to his black and climbed into the saddle, gritting his teeth as pain coursed through his left thigh. He rode down the slope to the rocks and slid out of the saddle to check the two Big S riders. Both men were dead.

He remounted and resumed following the track of the raiders, the jolting saddle giving his wound considerable trouble. After two miles he had to halt and dismount to rest his injured limb. He loosened the strip of cloth tied around the wound and blood oozed out of the torn flesh, so he retied the makeshift ligature, swung back into the torturous saddle and continued stoically.

By mid-afternoon he was certain that the raiders were making for Flat Ridge, and he pushed on at the black's fastest pace. The blankness of encroaching unconsciousness was never far from the periphery of his sight but the pain of his wound kept him upright in the saddle. He paused once to soak his thigh with tepid water from his canteen because the flesh seemed to be burning with a strange intensity and he wondered if he was being assailed by a fever.

But his alertness never wavered, and he reined in suddenly when he saw a change in the tracks he was following. One of the horses had become lame. He saw where it had been pulled up and the rider had dismounted to check its right foreleg. He checked the prints carefully. All six riders had veered off the trail until they found hard ground, but only five of them rode on in a different direction. The lame horse was still headed for Flat Ridge, its rider walking and leading the animal.

It was now early evening, and Chet was intent upon the prints of the single horse. He estimated that he was some four miles from town, and rode carefully, ready for any signs of an ambush. He was halfway up a long slope when his horse switched its ears forward, a sure sign that it had spotted someone ahead. The sun was low over in the west and the slanting rays made vision difficult. He eased his Winchester from its boot and cocked it, holding it ready for action. Then he spotted movement on the crest ahead.

A figure appeared and sunlight glinted on the barrel of a rifle. Chet saw the weapon being levelled in his direction and kicked his feet out of his stirrups. He ducked as the distant rifle fired, and heard the whine of a slug passing closely over his head. He paused only to fire a shot at the menacing figure before hurling himself from his saddle. The crash of his shot echoed as he hit the ground hard on his left shoulder. Pain flared in his leg but he ignored it and pushed himself up into a firing position, the muzzle of his rifle covering the spot where he had seen the ambusher.

The man was falling. Chet lifted his rifle, filled with grim satisfaction. He saw the man roll on the crest and then spring up and hurl himself into cover behind it. Chet pushed himself to his feet, favouring his injured leg, and stood with his rifle covering the spot where the man had disappeared, certain that he had scored a hit.

He climbed back into his saddle and finished his ascent of the slope, ready for trouble, but the ambusher had evidently fled. He slid his rifle into its boot as he neared the crest and drew his pistol. When he reached the top he found the spot where the man had fallen, and saw bloodstains on the grass. He looked around, picked out the tracks he had been following, and noted that they were still heading for the distant town. But now the man was riding the horse again, forcing the animal along despite its injury.

The tracks seemed never-ending, and shadows were creeping across the range when at last he sighted Flat Ridge in the distance. Yellow light was showing in some of the windows in the buildings when he followed the prints into the main street.

He looked around for a sight of tethered horses but the shadowed street was clear and he rode to the law office, which was in darkness. He reined in at the sidewalk and sat wondering where Decker had got to. A cooling breeze touched his hot cheeks as he decided to leave the prints for the time being and turned his mount to make for the doctor's house, where he slid out of his saddle and wrapped his reins around a post. He tottered a few steps because his left leg refused to take his weight and, falling against the door of the house, he had difficulty remaining on his feet.

Doc Pryce answered Chet's knock, his wounded shoulder heavily bandaged and his arm in a sling. Pryce frowned when he took in Chet's appearance.

'You look like you tangled with a bear and came off second best,' Pryce observed. 'Where have you been? I heard you took out after Sharman this morning. Did you catch up with that shyster?'

'Him and a few others,' Chet said through his clenched teeth.

'Come on in and I'll get Mrs Froy to attend to your leg. The ladies in town are taking turns to stand by in here and assist in the treatment of any patients who show up.'

'I'm surprised to see you on your feet.' Chet limped into the house and made for the doctor's office while Pryce called for his female assistant. A middle-aged woman of ample proportions appeared as Chet removed his gun belt and sat down heavily on a chair. She tut-tutted at the sight of the bloodstain on his thigh.

'Drop your pants, Chet,' Pryce ordered, and Chet complied.

Pryce examined the wound. 'We can clean that up,' he said. 'Get some hot water, Mrs Froy.' He opened a drawer in a cabinet and produced a bottle of whiskey and a glass as she departed. 'You look like you could do with a drink,' he observed, pouring a liberal tot into the glass. 'Get this down your neck and then lie down on that couch. We'll soon have you good as new. So where is Sharman? Did you catch up with him?'

'He's dead.' Chet drank the whiskey and then stretched out on the couch. He closed his eyes and tried to relax but Pryce kept asking questions which Chet would not answer.

Mrs Froy returned with a bowl of water and cleaned and dressed Chet's wound under the doctor's directions. Chet bore the woman's ministrations stoically and thanked her when she had completed the task.

'You should rest that limb for twenty-four hours, Chet,' Pryce observed.

'Like you rested your shoulder when you were shot,' Chet countered. 'Sorry, Doc, but I've got things to do.' He arose from the couch, pulled up his pants, and buckled his gun belt around his waist. 'How is Burt now?'

'He's making progress. He was awake

for some hours today, and kept asking about you. Have you got time to see him now?'

'I can make time,' Chet responded.

'Then go up and see him. The sight of you might settle him and he needs to get a good night's sleep.'

Chet mounted the stairs, favouring his left leg. The wound seemed easier but throbbing pain gripped the limb whenever he put his full weight upon it. He entered Burt's room to find his brother propped up in bed. Burt was conscious, his eyes half-open as Chet paused beside him. A faint smile touched his lips when he saw Chet.

'How are you doin', Burt?' Chet demanded, noting the pallor in his brother's cheeks and the feverish glint in his restless gaze.

'It's good to see you, Chet. Doc told me you were here last night but I don't recall seeing you.'

'I was here. I got in from Montana late yesterday and dropped in at the ranch. Dave Sawtell was there. Sue put him in as a caretaker when you were shot.' He said nothing about Sawtell's subsequent death. 'You're looking a lot better now. So what's been happening around here? What kind of trouble came up? Have you got any idea who shot you?'

Burt shook his head. 'I don't remember a thing about the shooting. All I can recall is leaving town that night and then waking up in here some days later.'

'Don't worry about it. Cast your mind back to the evening you were shot. Who did you see? Did you have trouble with anyone at that time?'

'I had a few drinks; that's all. I spoke to some of the men in from the neighbouring ranches and the talk was always about trouble on the range. I don't remember any trouble that evening.'

'So why did you get me back here?' Chet persisted. He had decided not to tell Burt about the trouble he had walked into since his arrival. There would be time later to bring Burt up to date on those events.

'Most of our cattle were rustled.' A shadow crossed Burt's pale face. 'I followed tracks but they petered out and I came up against a dead end. I knew other ranchers were losing stock but I didn't take much notice of what was going on until it happened to me. Then it was too late to stop the rot. A bunch of men had taken to riding the range at night. They came through Flying W twice, shooting up the place, but if they thought they could scare me out then they made a big mistake. I told myself they would have to kill me to make me quit.' A shadow crossed his face. 'And they came damn close to doing just that.'

'Didn't you get a look at those raiders? You must have seen someone or even a horse you could recognize!'

'No. They came at night, and I was too busy ducking lead to worry about who was doing the shooting.'

'So you sent for me.' Chet could see

Burt getting excited and was concerned for his brother's peace of mind.

'Sue put a lot of pressure on me to do so. She felt that as you owned half the spread you had a right to be here to face the trouble.'

Chet grimaced. He could well imagine what Sue had said. 'What went wrong between you and Sue?' he asked. 'I was surprised when I learned you two hadn't got hitched. The reason I cleared out five years ago was to give you a better chance of settling down.'

'I guess I got that situation dead wrong, Chet.' Burt spoke in a rueful tone. 'I thought Sue loved me, but after you left and I began to make a play for her she made it plain that I wasn't the man for her. In fact she seemed upset that you had cleared out, and I'm real sorry I stepped in between you two. You should never have gone away. I was the one who should have pulled stakes.'

'Forget about it,' Chet advised. 'All that happened a long time ago. I realize now that I needed to get away when I did. It sure helped me face facts and get a good line on what I wanted to do. I've put it all behind me, Burt, and you should try and do the same.'

'Have you heard that Hank Bartram was bush-whacked six months ago?' Burt asked.

'Yeah, I got the news. So what can you tell me about Circle B? Rafe Colby was working in the Red Dog saloon as a gambler when I pulled out. How did he come to marry Alice and take over the Bartram spread?'

Burt shook his head. He lifted a hand and motioned to the small table beside the bed. 'Give me a drink, Chet, will you? I'm burning up. Doc tells me I need to drink a lot of water.'

Chet complied, and lifted Burt's head to enable his brother to imbibe. Burt drank noisily and then flopped back on the pillow.

'I've still got a long way to go,' he said harshly. 'You asked about Colby, Chet.' He shook his head. 'He's a bad man if ever there was one. I was over to

181

Circle B quite a lot after you went off, and saw Colby there most evenings. He threw over his job at the saloon and worked on Alice until she agreed to marry him. You know how strange Alice was in those days. She wouldn't even look at a man, but she went overboard for Colby, and I could never understand why because he was too smooth, too overbearing. More than once I got an itch to bust him on the jaw, and Sue had to step between us one evening. It was then that Sue began to tell me about Colby's behaviour at the ranch.'

Burt's voice had lifted a couple of notches as tension filled him and Chet placed a restraining hand on his brother's shoulder.

'Take it easy, Burt,' he advised. 'You better stop talking if it is gonna upset you.'

'I'm all right. You watch out for Colby, Chet. He wrapped Hank Bartram around his little finger. Hank set him to work at the ranch keeping accounts, and Colby sure worked himself into a comfortable niche. Sue told me Hank even had arguments with Alice because she was slow accepting Colby's proposal of marriage, and when Alice eventually gave in and tied the knot with Colby there were big changes at Circle B.'

'I saw Alice and Colby in town earlier,' Chet admitted, 'and I didn't like the way Colby treated Alice.' His eyes narrowed as he recalled the scene on the trail earlier when Sue had left him to join her sister and Colby, who had been talking to Sharman. Colby had used his hands to cow both sisters, and Sharman had slunk off like a scared dog. 'I reckon I'll have to find the time to ride out to Circle B and have a long talk with Sue.'

Burt closed his eyes and Chet changed his mind about asking more questions.

'Get some sleep, Burt,' he advised. 'I'll see you again in the morning. Right now I need to get some grub. It has been kind of a long, hard day, and I've still got things to do.'

Burt shook his head and opened his eyes. 'I'm too restless to sleep,' he said. 'My thoughts are going around in my head like a mad bull in a corral. No matter which way I turn the situation over I come up against a rock wall. Sometimes I think I'm on the right track to finding answers but then it all slips away from me.'

'OK!' Chet sat down on the side of the bed. 'I'll ask some questions and you just try to find the answers, huh?'

'Fire away.' Burt lifted an unsteady hand to his forehead.

Chet studied his brother's lined face for a few moments before speaking. 'Tell me about some of the men around here,' he said at length. 'It seems a lot of strangers have moved into the county while I've been gone. Floyd Carson for instance! Who does he hang around with when he's in town?'

Burt frowned. 'What makes you ask about him?' he demanded. 'He's a hellion, and picked up with some more of his ilk around the county. I never had anything to do with him because I ain't the type to give anyone trouble, but his bunch went out of their way to upset folk.'

'So name the bunch,' Chet persisted.

'Danny Stockton and Owen Kenton the banker's son were Floyd's main pards, and Clark Sharman, the lawyer's son, started going around with them and getting into scrapes. What's on your mind, Chet? Have you had a run-in with them?'

'I'm just curious,' Chet replied. 'I need to feel my way around this situation until I get a complete picture in my mind. I heard that someone tried to buy Flying W. Who was that?'

'Vince Sharman came out to the spread one day with a low offer from some out-of-town combine which was interested in buying land around the county. I told him if he showed up again I'd take a gun to him, and he took the hint. But my trouble really started after I ran him off. Do you think he knows something about this crooked business?'

'Don't worry your head about that side of it, Burt.' Chet stood up, suppressing a groan as he put weight on his injured leg. 'I'll look in on you again but right now I need to get some grub. You concentrate on getting on your feet again and then we'll start fighting whoever is responsible for what's been happening around here.' He paused, thinking over Burt's answers. 'You mentioned Clark Sharman,' he mused. 'I don't recall that Vince Sharman had a son.'

'Yeah, Clark lived back East with his mother. He showed up around here after you'd gone. He was a lawyer in New England before he came West. I never did cotton to him. He worked with his father but got in with Floyd and his bunch.'

Burt sighed and closed his eyes. Chet watched his brother's face for some moments before turning away, and his own features were grim as he departed. He took his leave of Doc Pryce and limped along the street to the livery barn, leading his horse and favouring his leg. He could hear music coming from the Red Dog saloon, and bright light showed from its large windows, but most of the main street was in darkness except for the store, where figures were still going in and out.

A lantern hanging over the wide doorway of the barn threw a small circle of light on the ground directly below its position, and the shadows beyond it were impenetrable. Chet dropped his hand to the butt of his pistol as he paused at the water trough and waited while the black drank its fill. He looked around, his narrowed gaze probing the shadows, his ears strained for unnatural sound. He had no idea yet what he was up against, but sensed that the odds were too great for him to take any chances.

A figure appeared in the doorway of the barn and paused in the circle of light from the overhead lamp. Chet half-drew his pistol before he recognized the liveryman, Mitch Grover.

'Chet Walker,' Grover observed. 'Where have you been all day? The town has been real quiet since you rode out. Your homecoming sure was noisy, huh? How many men did you kill this morning? There were three that I heard about.'

'You don't know the half of it,' Chet replied.

'And I'll bet you don't know there's a couple of hardcases in town looking for you,' Grover replied. 'They showed up early this afternoon, and I was present in the Red Dog when they were asking about you. Someone told them you rode out of town earlier, and those two gunnies have been prowling around the street ever since, waiting for you to get back. And I'll tell you something else. This evening one of them came into the barn behind Ben Carson. I was up in the loft and heard them talking. It sounded like Carson hired those two gunnies to put you down for killing Floyd.'

Chet stiffened at the news and a sigh gusted from him. 'So that's how Carson means to play it, huh?' he mused. 'I had a feeling he wouldn't take Floyd's death lying down. Is he still in town?'

'No. He rode out quick, and those two guys are just waiting for you to show up.'

'Thanks for the warning, Mitch. Have you any idea where those two are right now?'

'One was in the restaurant when I was there for my supper half an hour ago. The other was in the saloon. When I was coming back here I saw them changing places, so one is still in the eating-house and the other is in the Red Dog.'

'Describe them,' Chet said curtly. 'I got things to do right now, but I'll need to get those two out of my hair.'

'I'll do better than that,' Grover said. 'Put your horse in a stall and I'll walk along the street with you and point those two out. But you got to promise not to let on that I told you about them, if things go wrong.'

'Thanks, Mitch. I appreciate your

help.' Chet led his black into the barn and Grover pitched some hay into a manger while Chet unsaddled the horse. 'Have you seen Decker around this evening?'

'No.' Grover shook his head. 'He came in for his horse this morning and rode out of town looking like he had somewhere important to go. He never said anything about his business, but then he always was close-mouthed. He ain't liked much around here, and I think he's too stupid to wear a deputy badge. He's made a lot of mistakes, and everyone around town wonders why the sheriff keeps him on the payroll.'

'And Abe Curry is away,' Chet observed.

'Sure, and if he had any sense he wouldn't come back to the mess we've got on our hands.'

With the needs of his horse taken care of, Chet hitched up his gun belt and eased his Colt in its holster. He led the way out of the stable and Grover kept to the shadows as they traversed the street. They reached the saloon and Grover approached the big window beside the batwings, rubbing dust from the pane before craning forward to view the interior of the long room.

'Take a look.' Grover's voice trembled with sudden excitement. 'Bill Twitchett, the bartender, is talking to one of those galoots right now. The guy in the red shirt is the man who was in the barn earlier, talking with Ben Carson.'

Chet peered through the window and saw almost a dozen men standing at the bar with several more sitting at the small tables dotted around the long room. His narrowed gaze flitted across the smoky scene, pausing for a brief second on a table in a far corner where four men were seated, and he recognized Henry Kenton the banker among those present. His gaze moved on until it rested on the big man at the bar wearing a red shirt, and studied his appearance. The man looked like a gunnie. He wore his pistol tied down on his right hip, and although he was in deep conversation with the bartender his eyes showed a restlessness which came with high alertness. He was keeping his surroundings under close observation, and his right hand did not stray far from the black butt of his holstered pistol.

'What are you gonna do about him, Chet?' Grover asked, suddenly nervous. 'If you're gonna face him then you better do it right now, before his sidekick shows up. You'll stand more chance taking them separately.'

Chet nodded. He had already decided to take advantage of the situation. 'You know what the other guy looks like, Mitch,' he said softly. 'Just give a whistle if you see him coming towards the saloon while I'm inside, huh?'

'I sure will, Chet! But make it quick.'

Chet nodded and moved to the batwings. He shouldered through the swing doors and stepped into the saloon, his right hand down at his side. He was conscious of the sudden silence that dropped over the long room like a cloak when he was spotted. The man in the red shirt swung around instantly to face the batwings and stepped away from the bar, his tall figure stiffening into full alertness. Chet saw the bartender speak urgently to the gunman before ducking out of sight behind the bar.

9

Chet paused twelve feet in front of the motionless gunman, keenly aware of the tension building up in the room. For a seemingly endless moment the complete silence was taut, pitched at an intolerable level, and then there was sudden frantic movement as the watching men moved swiftly to get out of the line of fire. Boots pounded the wooden floor and men jostled one another in their frantic haste. Apart from Chet, only the gunman did not move. His dark eyes were filled with sharp points of light, his right hand frozen in a ready-to-draw position just above the flared butt of his pistol. Yet a strange eagerness seemed to grip him, reminding Chet of a hound dog straining at a leash.

'I hear you've been looking for me,' Chet said in a low tone.

'I am if you're Chet Walker.'

'I'm Walker. Where's Ben Carson?'

'Who in hell is Ben Carson?'

'You were talking to him in the livery barn this afternoon, and my name was mentioned.'

'So that's Ben Carson. Yeah, we talked some.'

'And what's your name? What do you want on your tombstone?'

Tiny beads of sweat suddenly broke out on the gunnie's bronzed forehead and his hard expression changed imperceptibly. His eyes flickered, and Chet guessed he was hoping for the timely arrival of his sidekick. He had expected to catch his victim cold, with his gun pard at his side, but he had been caught alone, and his experience warned him that he did not have the edge.

'You've got a choice,' Chet said softly. 'Raise your hands and I'll take your gun, or you can reach for it and start the play.'

Time seemed to stretch out to

infinity. Chet waited, keyed up for action. He saw indecision show fleetingly on the gunnie's face, to be replaced by a shadow of fear that was quickly gone. The next instant the man snatched at his gun, his movement jerking a quick response from Chet. Steel rasped against leather, and then the silence was shattered by a double detonation that blasted through the long room almost as a single shot. Gun smoke flew, enveloping both men, and gun thunder rattled the bottles lined up on the back of the bar.

Chet stood motionless, his pistol levelled and a dribble of gun smoke curling from the muzzle. The gunman remained rigid for a moment, his gun clear of leather but still pointing downwards, his bullet embedded in the floor to the right of Chet's left foot. A splotch of blood appeared in the centre of the gunman's chest where Chet's bullet had struck home.

The man collapsed suddenly as his life ran out of his stiff body. He folded at the knees, waist and neck before tumbling to the floor like a discarded doll. The thunderous gun echoes faded and tension seeped away.

Movement came back to the saloon. Men pushed forward to stare down at the dead gunnie. A whistle sounded just outside the batwings and then heavy footsteps pounded on the sidewalk. Chet turned to face the doors, his gun in his hand but down at arm's length. Gun smoke tasted bitter against his teeth. A figure appeared — a dark face peering over the doors, and then a man thrust his way into the saloon and paused on the threshold, his right hand grasping the butt of his holstered gun.

'Don't pull your gun,' Chet called, cocking his pistol and levelling it.

The man froze. His gaze dropped to the dead man sprawled on the floor and disbelief crossed his taut features as he screwed up his eyes as if to discount the evidence of his sight.

'What happened here?' he demanded hoarsely.

'Is he your pard?' Chet countered.

'He's the other gunnie,' Mitch Grover called from the batwings. 'You got him dead to rights, Chet.'

'Chet Walker?' The gunman lifted his hand away from his gun in token of surrender and Grover came through the batwings to snatch the pistol out of the man's holster.

Chet went forward, and as he reached the gunnie's side Lance Decker looked in over the batwings.

'What's going on?' the deputy demanded, frowning at Chet. 'I had just left those four stiffs you killed this morning with Milner the undertaker when I heard shots.'

'You're just in time to throw this guy in a cell,' Chet replied. 'Can you get a posse together?'

'What, now?' Decker grimaced. 'Hell, I've been on the trail all day. What do you want with a posse?'

'There are some men around town I need to pull in for questioning, and the sooner they are behind bars the sooner we'll get at the truth.'

'OK. Give me five minutes and I'll be ready.' Decker drew his gun and grasped the gunnie by the shoulder. 'Come with me, mister. You can take a look at the inside of my jail.'

'I'm one of the regulars who turn out when a posse is needed,' Grover said. 'And so is Pete McFee, the blacksmith.' He indicated a big muscular man standing in the background 'How can we help you, Chet? Who do you want to arrest? What have you learned about the trouble since you got back last night?'

'Just back me,' Chet said. 'There'll be time for questions and answers later.' He looked around the saloon at the intent faces of the spectators. 'I see Kenton the banker over there,' he observed. 'Is his son Owen around?'

'That's Owen Kenton sitting at the table opposite his father,' Grover said.

'Let's take them in for questioning.' As Chet led the way to the corner table he reached into his breast pocket, produced his deputy marshal badge and pinned it to his shirt.

'I'll take Henry Kenton,' he said in an aside to Grover. 'You watch the others.'

He threaded his way between the tables and paused beside the chair where the banker was seated. Henry Kenton glanced up at him, and shock appeared on his taut features when he saw the law badge on Chet's shirt front.

'Henry Kenton,' Chet said. 'I need to talk to you. Get up and accompany me to the law office.'

'Who are you?' Owen Kenton demanded, pushing back his chair. He swayed as he got to his feet and his right hand eased up inside his coat to a shoulder holster.

'Don't draw on me,' Chet advised. 'Get both your hands in plain view and keep them there. You can come along with your father. Are you packing a gun?'

'Do as he says, Owen.' Henry Kenton got to his feet. 'I'm not armed, Marshal.'

Owen Kenton shrugged and let his

right hand fall to his side. 'I've got a .38 in a shoulder holster,' he admitted.

Chet reached under Owen's coat and, as he withdrew the gun, Owen staggered and then pitched sideways to the floor.

'What's wrong with him?' Chet demanded. 'Is he ill?'

'He's bleeding,' Grover observed, and bent over the unconscious man. He dragged open Owen's coat to reveal a patch of blood seeping through a bandage around the left shoulder.

'I shot someone who ambushed me about four miles out of town,' Chet said. 'I didn't get a good look at him but he was so desperate he rode his lame horse into town.'

'Owen brought his horse to me about half an hour ago,' McFee said. 'The animal was lame and Owen was favouring his shoulder. I saw blood on his coat.'

'That's good enough for me.' Chet nodded. 'OK. Let us get along to the law office.'

'What's this about?' Henry Kenton demanded.

'I'll tell you in the law office,' Chet said quietly. 'Get moving.'

Grover and McFee picked up Owen Kenton and carried him out of the saloon, followed by Henry Kenton. Chet walked behind the banker with his gun in his hand. A crowd of silent townsmen followed them from the saloon and, when they entered the law office Grover closed the door against the crowd.

Decker was standing behind his desk. The gunnie he had brought into the office was seated on a chair placed before the desk. Decker grimaced when he saw Henry Kenton and the now semi-conscious Owen Kenton, who was put into a chair.

'What's this all about?' Decker demanded of Chet. 'I can understand you pulling Henry Kenton in because of Matt Lawson, but what do you want with Owen?'

'Lock that gunnie and Owen in cells,'

Chet said. 'I want to talk to Henry Kenton first.'

Owen began to protest but Decker dragged him to his feet and pushed him towards the door leading into the cells. The gunman, menaced by Grover, followed behind. Chet waited until the connecting door had closed on them before turning his attention to Henry Kenton.

'You know why I've brought you in,' Chet said. 'You let Sharman use your horse this morning to get away from me, and when I followed him you sent Matt Lawson out to kill me. Is that right?'

'I don't know what you're talking about.' Henry Kenton shook his head emphatically. 'I didn't know Lawson had left town, so his subsequent actions are not my responsibility.'

'Lawson is dead, but he told me a different story before he passed on.' Chet decided to try a bluff. 'He told me he was working for the Kansas Land and Cattle Combine, that you were

203

doing some work for them, and you sent him out to kill me. I've got it figured that the Kansas Land and Cattle Combine are behind the trouble. They have been buying up land in the county, and scaring out ranchers who did not want to sell. I suspect that they are responsible for the murder of Hank Bartram and the ambush of my brother last week. Sharman is dead. He was involved in the land deals that were pushed through, and I believe you were working with him.'

'This is preposterous!' Kenton shook his head. 'I have never heard such nonsense. I have had no dealings with any out-of-town combine. And why have you arrested my son? Owen is not mixed up in anything.'

'He rode around with Floyd Carson and several other young men who were known hell-raisers,' Chet said. 'I killed Carson when Flying W was raided last night and your son was probably riding with him on that raid. Danny Stockton was another who rode around with

Floyd Carson, but he was killed at the Big S ranch today along with his father. Half a dozen raiders rode in there shooting and helling, and I trailed that bunch right back here to town. I'm pretty certain now that your son Owen was one of those raiders and I'm gonna hold him while I check on his movements over the past twenty-four hours. I'm holding you until I've had a chance to look at your paperwork at the bank to see who bought those ranches which were sold in the past few months.'

'You're barking up the wrong tree.' Kenton shook his head. 'I want a lawyer.'

'I killed the only shyster in town,' Chet countered.

'Then bring one in from Kansas City.'

Decker and Grover returned from the cells and Chet motioned to Henry Kenton.

'Lock him up and bring Owen Kenton out here,' he said.

Henry Kenton protested loudly as he was removed to the cells. Owen came back and sat down heavily. His face was pale, his eyes showing pain, and he stared fixedly at the floor. Chet watched him for some moments.

'You were with the raiders who hit Flying W last evening,' Chet said suddenly, and Owen jerked up on his seat.

'That's a lie,' he responded. 'I was here in town all evening, and I know several men who can back me up.'

'You were out riding today. I followed your tracks all the way from Big S. Why was Danny Stockton killed? He was one of your pards. Was there a falling out or did the people you work for want the Big S ranch?'

'I wasn't out on the range today.' Owen did not look up from the floor. 'I was in my office at the bank from eight o'clock this morning until closing time.'

'I made a note of the tracks I followed back to town,' Chet persisted. 'The rider I was trailing ambushed me because his horse had gone lame, but I managed to crease him with a slug. The prints of that lame horse led straight into town, and I have a witness who saw you ride in on a lame horse and noticed blood on you. Who bandaged your shoulder? Did you go to Doc Pryce?'

'I wasn't shot. My horse reared up from a rattlesnake. I fell off and hit my shoulder on a rock. You got nothing on me.'

Decker stood in front of Owen and grasped the front of the youngster's shirt. He half-lifted Owen out of his seat and held him for some moments before allowing him to slump back.

'Let me take him in a cell for a few minutes,' Decker said. 'I'll get the truth out of him.'

'No. Lock him up and bring that gunnie out. I'll check Owen's horse shortly. I know its prints, and I have no doubt that he was the man I shot. He'll start talking when I lay some evidence before him.'

Decker half-dragged Owen Kenton

into the cells and returned a few moments later with the disconsolate gunnie. Chet pointed to the chair set before the desk and motioned for the man to sit down.

'What's your name?' Chet demanded.

'Hank Stowe.'

'Who paid you to kill me?'

'I haven't been paid to kill anyone.' Stowe shrugged his shoulders. 'I'm spending a few days in town before I look around for a riding job.'

'Show me your hands,' Chet commanded.

Stowe looked at Chet for several moments before holding out his hands, palms upward. Chet shook his head.

'You've never worked cattle in your life. You live by your gun.'

'You're gonna have to prove that,' Stowe responded.

'That won't be too difficult.' Chet relaxed. 'OK, put him back behind bars. I'll check out Owen Kenton's horse now. What happened to the animal, McFee?'

'It's still in my forge,' the blacksmith replied. 'Owen told me to put it in his father's barn behind the bank when I'd finished with it.'

Decker came back into the office. He was scowling.

'I wouldn't treat them so leniently,' he said. 'I'd get the truth out of them.'

'That's not the way to do it,' Chet replied. 'We'll let them sweat until morning. By then I hope to have some evidence against them. Come on, McFee; let's go take a look at that lame horse. Then I'm gonna get something to eat. You'll make arrangements for the office to be covered if you leave it, Decker?'

'Sure. Ed Barnes is the night jailer when we have anyone behind bars. He'll be showing up shortly.'

Chet left the office with McFee and they walked along the street to the blacksmith's shop. McFee lit a lantern and led the way to a stall at the rear of the forge where a horse was standing.

'The shoe on the right hoof was loose

and had twisted,' McFee explained. 'I took it off and found the fetlock bruised so I'll put a new shoe on him in the morning.'

Chet took the lantern and went outside the street door. He dropped to one knee over some prints and studied them. McFee watched him intently.

'They are the prints made by Owen Kenton's horse when I led him inside,' he said.

'And they are the ones I followed all the way to town from Big S.' Chet nodded. 'So Owen has got some explaining to do. I wonder who the other five riders were. They left him when Owen's horse went lame. I'll have to ride out of town tomorrow and pick up their trail. It should be a simple matter to track them down.'

'Everyone knows the bunch Owen Kenton rides around with,' McFee said. 'You killed one of them last night — Floyd Carson; another died today out at Big S — Danny Stockton. Clark Sharman, the lawyer's son is another, but I haven't seen him around for a few days. Is that enough to be going on with?'

'Thanks.' Chet nodded. 'I'll have them rounded up and find out what they've got to say. I have enough to hold Owen in jail, and I reckon he'll start talking when he realizes he's mixed up in murder.'

He left the forge and walked back along the street to the eating-house, his thoughts busy on the situation, and he was satisfied that he had made a big breakthrough. But he still had a long way to go, for there were holes in the picture he was creating in his mind. He ate supper, and a waitress came from the kitchen to pause at his table.

'I'm Ann Teasdale,' she said. 'You've just been pointed out to me. You're Chet Walker.'

Chet nodded. 'Can I help you?' he asked.

'I served those two gunnies in here earlier. They came in at different times but they both asked if you were around.

211

They looked like bad trouble.'

'Thanks for the warning.' Chet smiled. 'Would you be prepared to swear in court that you heard them asking for me?'

'Yes. I also saw Ben Carson in here talking to one of those men, and he handed over some money.'

'We'll talk some more about this later,' Chet said. 'Thanks for coming forward.'

He left the restaurant and went back to the law office. Decker was at his desk, writing laboriously and sweating over his reports.

'I'm ready to talk to Owen Kenton again,' Chet said.

'I'll fetch him out.' Relief showed on Decker's face as he got to his feet and went into the cells.

Owen Kenton was again brought into the office. He was pale, his eyes showing pain. He slumped into the chair before the desk.

'I've got nothing to say,' Owen said before Chet could speak.

'I'm charging you with shooting at me this afternoon,' Chet told him. 'I know you were with the group of men who rode into the Big S yard and gunned down Joe Stockton and his son Danny so I'm holding you on suspicion of murder. Have you got anything to say in answer to those charges?'

'You've got the wrong man.'

'I'll prove the truth of those charges before I'm through,' Chet concluded.

Owen Kenton was taken back to his cell. The street door opened and a tall man carrying a double-barrelled shotgun entered the office.

'I'm Ed Barnes,' he said. 'I hear you've got some customers behind bars.'

'You're the night jailer.' Chet nodded.

'I always take a turn around the street before I come on duty,' Barnes said, 'in case someone is planning to hit the jail and turn the prisoners loose. I was near the livery barn when three riders came in from the range. When they passed under the lantern in the doorway of the barn I recognized one of them as Ben Carson. It could be he's come in to find out what happened to you.'

Chet drew his pistol instantly and checked the weapon. He was reloading an empty chamber when Decker emerged from the cells.

'I heard that,' Decker said. 'We better pick up Carson and get his angle on what happened earlier.'

'I'll handle it,' Chet said softly. 'I don't want to have to kill Ben Carson unless I have to. I can understand how he is feeling right this minute. I'll try and bring him in alive.'

'It'll be a two-man job if Carson has got a couple of his riders with him,' Decker insisted.

Before Chet could answer, a pistol boomed outside the office and a bullet smashed through the door. It clanged against the stove before burying itself in the back wall of the office.

'Come on out, Walker,' Ben Carson called through the fading echoes of the shot. 'I'm gonna kill you for shooting my boy.'

10

Chet moved quickly towards the door leading to the cells, motioning for Decker to accompany him.

'Let me out the back door,' Chet said. 'You can talk to Carson from the office while I sneak along the alley to the street and get the drop on him.'

Decker nodded. There was no time to argue. Chet left the jail by the side door and went swiftly along the alley to the street end, pistol in hand. He halted in the darkness and eased forward to peer into the shadows surrounding the jail. A moment later he heard Decker calling from inside the front office.

'Carson, you're making a big mistake. Chet Walker ain't here. Come on in and check us out.'

'I know he's in there,' Carson replied. 'Send out that murdering skunk.'

215

Chet could see nothing, but pinpointed the voice as coming from an alley opposite the law office. He waited to get Carson's reaction to Decker's invitation, which came swiftly. A tongue of red-yellow flame spurted from the opposite alley mouth and three bullets smacked into the front of the office. Echoes raced across town and shattered glass tinkled on the sidewalk. Chet cocked his gun.

The next instant three figures appeared from the alley mouth and started across the street, firing as they approached. Slugs tore into the law office. Chet drew a bead on Ben Carson, aimed low, and fired. Carson jumped, twisted, and fell to the ground. His two companions turned their guns on the spot where Chet was standing.

Decker opened fire from the office and one of the two men fell heavily. The other turned to dart back to cover and Decker fired again, to send him flying head first into the dust. Chet moved out from the alley, covering Carson.

Lamplight from the law office bathed the rancher, and Chet saw him lift a pistol into the aim.

'Drop it, Carson,' Chet called. 'You'll never make it.'

Carson bared his teeth in a snarl of defiance. His gun lifted and swung to cover Chet. At the same instant Decker fired from the doorway of the law office. Carson pitched over backwards and lay still. Gun echoes faded sullenly across the town.

Chet moved out to where Carson lay. The C7 rancher was dead, his face contorted in hatred and grief. Decker came out of the law office and strode to Chet's side.

'I didn't think you would shoot him so I did,' Decker said. 'He was never gonna give up. You killed his son and he wanted you to pay for that. He's better off where he's gone. He wouldn't ever get over losing Floyd. The pity is, if he'd reared the youngster properly — taught him right from wrong — Floyd would have been a credit to him.'

Silence returned to the street. Chet reloaded the empty chambers in his pistol as he turned to the law office, but at that moment a shot sounded along the street. Chet paused in mid-stride, swinging to face the sound, and frowned as echoes chased across the town. A woman screamed in a shrill, high tone of fear, and the ragged sound was cut off suddenly, as if a hand had been clapped across her mouth.

'What the hell!' Decker cursed. 'Now what's going on?'

He ran along the street in the direction of the disturbance and Chet went with him. The sound of running horses came clearly out of the darkness ahead, leaving town in a hurry. A group of men were emerging from the Red Dog saloon and Chet halted in front of them, breathing hard.

'Did anyone see what happened?' he demanded.

'I was standing out here having a quiet smoke,' someone said. 'A woman came into town on a horse with two men chasing her. They caught up with her just out here and she turned on them with a pistol. She shot one of them and the other grabbed her. Then they rode out. The man she shot was sagging in his saddle and I don't think he'll get very far.'

'Did you get a look at the woman?' Decker demanded, coming up.

'No.' The witness shook his head. 'But I think I recognized her voice; she sounded like Sue Bartram of Circle B.'

A pang stabbed through Chet. Sue always carried a pistol. He recalled that she had argued with Rafe Colby on the trail that morning, and Colby had struck her before back-handing his wife Alice. He glanced around, saw a saddled horse standing hipshot at a nearby hitch rail, and ran to it.

'Whose horse is this?' he demanded.

'It's mine,' someone in the crowd replied.

'I'm borrowing it.' Chet tightened the cinch and swung into the saddle. The sudden movement put a strain on his left leg and sent a pang through his wound.

'Hey, Walker,' Decker called loudly. 'I'll get a posse together and follow you out to Circle B.'

Chet lifted a hand in acknowledgement as he spurred the horse along the street, reaching a gallop within a few yards. He narrowed his eyes as he left town and hit the darkness of the range. He strained his ears, listening for tell-tale sounds of the trio who had departed before him.

He slowed his pace until his eyes became accustomed to the night. There was no moon but plenty of starshine, and the trail to Circle B showed like a white ribbon before him. The horse was fast, and before long Chet caught a glimpse of movement ahead. He drew his pistol, urged the horse into a faster gait, and began to overhaul the lone rider.

The fleeing man heard the ominous sound of pursuit and swung his horse around to face his back trail. Chet lifted his pistol, watching for signs of resistance, but the man was clinging to his saddle horn, his head forward and his chin on his chest. As Chet moved in with upraised gun the man pitched sideways, kicked his feet clear of his stirrups and fell out of the saddle. Chet dismounted beside him, pistol ready.

The man was unconscious. Blood showed darkly on his shirt front. Chet disarmed him and straightened to glance around, listening intently for sounds of Sue and the other rider. He heard nothing but the soft breath of the sighing wind in his ears. He struck a match and bent over the inert figure, holding the tiny flame close to the upturned face. It took him but a moment to recognize the man as being one of the two gunmen who had ridden into town the previous night with Sue's party.

The man groaned and his eyelids flickered. The flame of the match died and Chet sat back on his heels. When the man tried to sit up, Chet grasped him.

'Lie still,' he advised. 'You're bad hurt. What's your name?'

'Chuck Hackett. That hell-cat Sue Bartram shot me.'

'Why were you and your pard chasing her?'

Hackett stifled a groan. 'She escaped from the ranch and Colby sent us to fetch her back. We caught up with her in town and she shot me before Farris could grab her.'

'You said Sue escaped from Circle B. Why was she being held prisoner?'

'She was giving Colby trouble and he locked her in the storeroom but she busted out and made for town.'

'And Farris is taking her back to Circle B?'

'That's the idea, unless she gets the better of him. She's a regular she-bear.'

'Can you make it back to town?' Chet asked. 'I'll put you back in your saddle if you think you can hang on.'

'Don't move me.' Hackett stifled a groan. 'I'm hard hit.'

'You and Farris tried to shoot me last

night,' Chet said. 'When Dave Sawtell was killed! It had to be you and your sidekick doing the shooting. Tell me about it, Hackett. You're on the way out, and it will be better for you to die with a clear mind.'

'Go to hell!' Hackett stifled a groan.

Chet got to his feet and swung into the saddle. He gazed down at the inert man for a moment before turning away and setting the horse into a run along the dark trail to the Circle B ranch. His face was grim and his eyes glinted in the starlight.

He had noticed the previous evening that the trouble that existed between Sue and Rafe Colby was of long standing. He figured pressure had built up in Sue because Colby had taken over running Circle B when Hank Bartram had been killed. But Colby had slapped Sue that morning on the trail, which was not good. Sue was not the type to take that kind of treatment lying down, and being locked in the storeroom at the ranch would have been the last straw for her in what had obviously become an intolerable situation. She must have been really wound up to take a gun to Hackett to avoid being dragged back to the ranch, and Chet wondered if there was anything more ominous in the background between the girl and Colby.

His thoughts meandered on as he followed the trail across a ridge and passed through a juniper thicket. The stars were bright and a thin crescent of the moon was showing now just above the eastern horizon. Night insects were in full song in the long grass. Chet realized that he was weary from the grim activities of the past day but the knowledge that Sue was in dire trouble bolstered his flagging energy and he rode fast, watching for signs of movement ahead on the shadowed trail.

He rode through a patch of scrub sage and breathed deeply of its pungent scent, alert for trouble, certain that Farris would not overlook the fact that he might be followed from town after the shooting there. Later, he topped a ridge and reined up to gaze at the distant lights showing on Circle B. He decided against riding in openly. There were a number of questions in his mind which he wanted to put to Rafe Colby, but, judging by Colby's general attitude the previous evening, Chet did not think the man would co-operate willingly.

Chet dismounted way out from the yard and walked the horse in closer. He did not doubt that in these troublesome times at least one guard would be watching the spread during the hours of darkness. He tethered the horse in a thicket about one hundred yards out and stood for a few moments to get his bearings. The silence was intense and nothing moved around him as he walked towards the huddled buildings of the ranch.

The rapid tattoo of approaching hoofs came to Chet's ears as he bent to slip under the top rail of the fence surrounding the yard. He froze and waited. Presently a single rider appeared and opened the main gate to pass through. Chet watched and waited. The rider went openly across the yard to the ranch house, and a moment later Chet heard a challenge being called from the dense shadows surrounding the porch.

'It's Clark Sharman,' the rider replied loudly. 'I've got to see Colby. My father ran from town this morning with a deputy marshal on his tail, and the only place he would head for is here.'

'We ain't seen hide or hair of him,' the guard replied. 'But come on in and talk to the boss.'

Chet eased between two rails and moved across the yard, keeping to the denser shadows. Clark Sharman dismounted by the porch and Chet saw his figure outlined briefly against the light shining from one of the front windows of the house. The door was opened and two figures entered the building. Chet made for a corner of the porch and moved into the dense shadows at the front of the house.

He risked a glance through a window and saw the guard and Clark Sharman standing in front of Rafe Colby, who was sitting at a desk in a corner. Farris was seated on a chair beside the desk, holding a pistol in his right hand, its muzzle pointing at the floor. The window was open and the voices of the men came clearly to Chet's ears.

'What do you mean, my father didn't show up here?' Clark Sharman demanded. 'He was chased out of town and had nowhere else to go. He must have come here.'

'You're calling me a liar!' Colby declared. 'I told you Vince didn't come here today. He probably kept riding till he was over the county line. I never knew a man more scared of his own shadow. He wasn't cut out for the kind of work he got involved in, and if he has pulled out then he's done us all a favour.'

'You'd toss him to the law now he's done your dirty work!' Clark said angrily. 'Is that all you care about the men who work for you? The least you could do is stand by them when they fall into trouble. Do you know that Chet Walker is a deputy marshal? And he's getting wise to what is going on, judging by what's been happening in Flat Ridge. This morning he killed those two gunnies you sent to get him, and this evening he arrested Henry and Owen Kenton. I guess it won't be long before he shows up here asking questions. If you don't start helping those who put their necks on the line for you then you won't get much further. It ain't good enough, Colby. My father has done a lot for you over the past two years. He eased you into where you are now, but your plans are coming unstuck. Ben Carson was killed in town this evening, and Joe and Danny Stockton were shot down on their porch earlier.'

Colby leaned back in his seat, eyes narrowed and displeasure showing on his face. He glanced at the motionless Farris, who straightened a little in his seat.

'Joe and Danny Stockton were getting too big for their boots,' Colby said. 'I had to teach them a lesson like I'm gonna have to do to some folks much closer to me. I got personal troubles to deal with at the moment and if Vince has got so scared he's run out then he's on his own. I've been trying to get him to grow some backbone but he's useless in the situation we've got coming up and if he ain't man enough to stand on his own two feet then he'll have to go to the wall.'

'I won't stand by and let that happen,' Clark said. 'If you won't help my father then I'll do whatever it takes to get him in the clear.'

'That sounds like a threat.' Colby leaned forward in his seat, rested his elbows on the desk and lowered his chin into his cupped hands. 'You've been making good dough out of my business for doing practically nothing, and now the time has come to do a bit more you're fixing to bite the hand that feeds you. I'll slap you down hard if I have to — you and all the others.'

'Do you want me to handle this?' Farris cut in. 'There'll be room in the buckboard for this whining skunk when we run it into the quicksand at Juniper Sinks with the women in it.'

'OK.' Colby nodded. 'Kill him, dump him in the buckboard, and then get Alice and Sue down here and stick them in with him. If you set out now for Juniper Sinks you should be back here by sunup.'

Farris jerked up his pistol and fired a single shot that struck Clark Sharman in the chest. The youngster was flung backwards by the impact of the bullet and crashed to the floor. Chet was shocked by the cold-blooded killing and lifted his pistol but refrained from taking action as he pondered Colby's reference to a buckboard and Juniper Sinks. It sounded as if Alice and Sue were in bad trouble. Somehow the women had finally fallen out with Rafe Colby.

Chet turned away and moved silently to the end of the porch. He made his way to the rear of the house, where a solitary lamp was burning in the big kitchen. A quick glance through the window showed him the kitchen was deserted and he went to the door, found it unbolted, and entered silently. The inner door of the kitchen was ajar and Chet, gun in hand, crossed to it and peered along the passage leading to the front of the house. He tiptoed to the stairs and mounted them slowly to discover a lamp burning on a small table in the upper passage which cast dim light against the ceiling.

Chet knew Sue had always used the far corner bedroom facing west and went to it. He tried the door, found it bolted on the outside, and opened it to discover the girl sitting on the edge of her bed, gazing into space.

'What's going on, Sue?' he demanded.

The girl uttered a cry and sprang to her feet. Her cheeks were tear-stained, and Chet saw a dark bruise on her left cheek. She threw herself into his arms and began to sob. Chet holstered his gun, took her by the shoulders and shook her gently. She gulped and looked up at him with big, rounded eyes.

'Colby said he had my father killed!' she gasped. 'Did you watch me this morning when I left you to join him and Alice? Vince Sharman was talking to them on the trail when I joined them, and he was in a bad state. He was terribly scared of you. I don't know what that shyster had been up to, but he said he couldn't stay in town until you had been removed. Colby said you would be taken care of, and when I argued with him he hit me. Alice took my part for once and he hit her also.'

'I saw that happening,' Chet said. 'So what happened after you took off from Colby?'

'We came back to the ranch with Colby following us and we both started on him when we reached here. Some real nasty things were said. In the end

Alice told Colby to pack his bags and leave. She was through with him. And that was when he told us he had arranged for Hank to be killed so he could take over the ranch, and he wasn't going to let two stupid girls run him off. He said he was playing for high stakes and Vince Sharman and Henry Kenton were working with him to take over the whole county. He bragged openly about the men that had been shot on his orders.'

'Did he mention the Kansas Land and Cattle Combine?' Chet asked.

'Alice asked Colby if he was working with the Combine because there has been a lot of talk about them around the county, but Colby said he and the Combine were business rivals, and he was using them to avert suspicion from himself. He locked Alice in her bedroom and put me in the storeroom but I escaped.'

'I was in town when you rode in with Hackett and Farris chasing you,' Chet said. 'You shot Hackett, and Farris brought you back here, huh?'

'Yes, and I heard Colby tell Farris to arrange an accident that will kill Alice and me. He said something about running a buckboard with us in it into the quicksand at Juniper Sinks.' Sue clutched at Chet's arm, her eyes wide in fear. 'Hackett and Farris shot Dave Sawtell in town last night. Colby said Dave was too friendly with you. I asked Colby about your brother Burt and he said not finishing Burt off was the worst mistake he'd made and he planned to put that right pretty soon. What can we do, Chet? How did you get in here?'

'The same way I'll get you out,' Chet replied. 'And you can take Alice with you. I'll set you on the trail to town.'

'What will you do? You can't fight the whole crooked bunch of them out here. Most of my father's outfit were fired when Colby took over.'

'I'll try to grab Colby and sneak him away from here before anyone knows what's happening,' Chet said. 'Let's turn Alice loose and get you clear before I make my play. Come on, there's no time to lose. Colby is fixing to ship you and Alice out pretty quick now. It looks like there's no limit to what he'll do to keep his crooked business rolling.'

The house was silent and still as Sue led the way to Alice's room. The door was bolted on the outside and Sue slid the bolt back, opened the door, and Alice came out of the room in a rush, ready to fight, her fingers hooked to claw at Chet.

'Steady on!' he cried, grasping her wrists. 'Save that for Colby.'

'Chet, it's you!' Alice subsided. 'Thank God! I've been praying for you to show up. I knew you would come. Has Sue told you about what's been going on here? Rafe has finally showed his true colours.'

'I've got enough of it to take Colby in,' Chet replied. 'But first I want to get you and Sue out. Follow me quietly and I'll set you on the trail to Flat Ridge.'

'I'm not going anywhere,' Alice said

firmly. 'I was duped by Rafe, and I'm not running out. He admitted having Hank killed and I'll see he pays for that. We'll settle this business right now.'

She turned and ran to the stairs. Sue went after her and grasped her arm.

'Be sensible, Alice,' she reproved. 'Colby won't give in without a fight and blood will be shed.'

Alice shook herself free of Sue's grasp and started down the stairs. Chet dashed after her, caught up with her in the ground-floor passage, but as he grasped her shoulder a gun blasted a single shot and echoes shook the house. Chet palmed his gun and stepped around Alice but she moved with him and ran to the door leading into the big front living-room.

Chet was two paces behind Alice when she thrust open the door and ran into the room. He followed hard on her heels and saw the guard lying on the floor beside Clark Sharman. There was a splotch of blood on the guard's shirt-front. Colby was standing before the big stone fireplace, a pistol dangling in his right hand, but Farris was not in the room. Chet grasped Alice's shoulder, intending to drag her out of the line of fire but Colby lifted his gun instantly. Chet thrust Alice aside and fired at Colby as Alice fell to the floor.

Colby was rattled by the sight of Chet looming in the doorway and his first shot went wide. Chet heard the bullet thud harmlessly into the woodwork around the door, but Colby staggered and blood appeared on his shirt at the right shoulder. He rocked back on his heels, struggled to lift his gun to continue shooting, and Chet squeezed his trigger again. The big pistol bucked in his hand, Colby spun around and fell on his face.

Sue pushed past Chet and dropped to her knees beside Alice. Tears were streaming down her cheeks until she discovered that her sister was not dead. The porch door was suddenly thrown open with great force and it crashed against the wall as Farris stepped into the house. Chet fired before the gunman could work his pistol, and Farris went down on one knee, a bullet in his chest. He used both hands to try and bring his gun to bear on Chet. Sue snatched up the gun Colby had dropped and fired three shots; all struck Farris and sent him toppling over on his back.

Gun smoke drifted across the big room. Chet drew a sharp breath which rasped in his throat. His mind was whirling as he reloaded the empty chambers in his deadly pistol. He suspected that the shooting would bring Colby's crooked crew running and prepared to continue the fight. The trouble was out in the open now and gun play would settle it once and for all.

He heard voices outside, the thud of approaching horses, and moved out to the porch, his pistol raised for action. Then he heard Lance Decker shouting orders to the posse he had brought out from town and sporadic gunfire blasted through the night as the law men cleaned up. Chet did not involve himself. He had enough evidence now to bring the whole crooked business to an end. He sheathed his gun.

Sue came to his side and clutched at his arm. He looked down into her tear-streaked face but she was smiling.

'I prayed for you to come home,' she said. 'I knew you were the only man who could settle this, and you've proved me right.'

'There is still a lot to do around here,' he responded, 'and I won't be leaving again. I gave up my job in Montana and took a deputy marshal badge in Kansas City so there's nothing up north for me any more. I reckon I'll settle back here where my roots are, and when time has a chance to work its healing process perhaps we'll be able to find a way out of the mess we got ourselves into.'

'I'm sure we shall.' Sue clung to his arm as Lance Decker came into the house to announce that all resistance had ended.

Chet slid his arm around Sue's slender shoulders, and for the first time in five years he felt optimistic about his future.

THE END

We do hope that you have enjoyed reading this large print book.

Did you know that all of our titles are available for purchase?

We publish a wide range of high quality large print books including:
**Romances, Mysteries, Classics
General Fiction
Non Fiction and Westerns**

Special interest titles available in large print are:
**The Little Oxford Dictionary
Music Book, Song Book
Hymn Book, Service Book**

Also available from us courtesy of Oxford University Press:
**Young Readers' Dictionary
(large print edition)
Young Readers' Thesaurus
(large print edition)**

For further information or a free brochure, please contact us at:
**Ulverscroft Large Print Books Ltd.,
The Green, Bradgate Road, Anstey,
Leicester, LE7 7FU, England.
Tel:** (00 44) **0116 236 4325
Fax:** (00 44) **0116 234 0205**

LIGHTNING AT THE HANGING TREE

Mark Falcon

Mike Clancey was the name inside the rider's watch, but many people during his travels called him Lightning. He was too late to stop a hanging, the men were far away when he reached the lonely swinging figure of a middle-aged man. Then a youth rode up and Lightning found out that the hanged man was his father. So why had he been hanged? Soon the two were to ride together in a pitiless search for the killers.